WWW.BirdFeedersMedia.com

ISBN 979-8-9879913-5-0

Published by Bird Feeders Media.

Produced in the U.S.A.

Ashley's Children: Quin High

By Drep Code

ASHLEY'S CHILDREN

Chapter 1: Being Blocked

To athletes, winning is the most important part of their sport.

Those who say otherwise are trying to fool you or themselves.

This is, at least, a strongly held belief for Quin High.

For Quin, having spent countless hours training and thousands of dollars, losing was unacceptable.

Quin's desire to win has grown even stronger now that he is competing to be part of a special wrestling team at Ward University. The chosen team members would soon compete against a rival university in their upcoming Contest of Combat Sports event. Being chosen for this team would boost Quin's chances of earning the scholarships he needs to continue attending Ward University and give him and his girlfriend something to look forward to during their upcoming spring break. He just needed to win the afternoon scrimmage match in the school's gymnasium against his opponent to qualify.

And win is what he did.

After an intense struggle against his opponent, Quin scored a pinfall victory. However, during the match, Quin obtained one of the biggest threats to a sports scholarship. An injury.

When the cheering spectators settled down, the pain in his left ankle became obvious to everyone when Quin struggled to walk away from the competing circle.

"Are you okay, Quin?" asked one of the monitoring athletic trainers.

"Nothing to see here coach! I'll just be in the locker room," Quin replied.

"Quin! Get back here!"

At the sound of his name, Quin limped faster until he entered the locker room. He sat on the bench, relieving the pain from standing on his injured ankle. While Quin pondered how to keep his injury a secret, the locker room door swooshed open from the trainer's pursuit of Quin.

"Stop running from me, Quin! Let me see that ankle!"

"Uh-oh, I was hoping no one noticed. Can we pretend like nothing happened?"

"No way, son! I'm taking you to the examining room to check that ankle."

After a series of ankle stares and harsh pokes in the examining room, the trainer explained Quin's situation.

"Looks like you have a second-degree ankle sprain. The good news is that you won't need surgery. I'll give you a CAM boot to help you recover and remain independent."

"I'm glad I'll still be able to shower," Quin replied. "Will I recover in time to make it to the contest?"

"No,"

"That's the bad news I wanted to avoid by running from you!"

"You'll be recovering for about 45 days. That means we have no choice but to replace you on the team so we can win."

As the trainer placed a CAM boot on Quin's left foot, Quin's head turned sideways in frustration. The thought of being replaced after winning fueled him with resentment. "I won yet I'm the loser!"

Quin lay on his dorm room bed pondering what spring break would entail with such an inconvenient injury. He needed to find an explanation for his girlfriend, May, since they had plans for the beach with some of her friends.

Quin feared that his relationship with May often felt like a dead end. When he pondered why she was in a relationship with him and not someone else, no meaningful answer came to mind. Habitually, Quin would disregard the topic by believing May wanted to get married as soon as possible—just as he did, but lately he began doubt that belief. Competing in the campus's rivalry match was a way for Quin to add more to their relationship, but now that opportunity was gone.

Quin's cell phone began ringing. It was May calling.

"Hey, May!"

"Quin? Someone posted a video of you limping. Looks like you hurt your foot."

"Would you believe me if I said it was photoshopped, ha- ha?"

"Oh, shut up. I'm on my way over."

"Feel free to take your time," Quin nervously suggested.

Quin hung up the phone, still unsure of what to do or say about the planned spring break trip.

After scrolling through social media posts, he hatched an idea.

He'd pretend to be well enough to attend the beach gathering and just wouldn't swim due to his injury. For improving their relationship, he would tell May that he planned to get a job soon and could get her a car by their sophomore year.

Quin disliked the idea of making a promise he might not keep, especially one as significant as buying May a car on his limited budget—yet it wouldn't be a lie if he actually succeeded.

Now that Quin knew what to tell May, he just had to wait until she arrived.

When May entered his room, a smile formed upon Quin's face. Despite having known May for years and having been in a relationship with her since high school, he was still always happy to see her. Being with her made Quin feel like the luckiest guy in the world.

May placed a chair near Quin's bed so he could continue lying down comfortably. After receiving a hug and food from May, Quin explained the story of his injured ankle.

"The good news is that I can still shower and take care of myself, so I don't need help with anything. And I can still go to the beach with you and your friends on spring break!" Quin exclaimed. "We can still have fun liked we planned."

"About that Quin—it's a good thing your ankle is hurt."

Quin stared with curiosity wondering how being injured could be good.

"Instead of going with my friends," May continued, "I'll be with the orphans I do volunteer work with."

"I think you're saying it would be easier to do that without me."

"Yes. Also, my new friend helped me find a new donor for the orphanage."

"New friend?"

"Annalisa. I met her a few weeks ago. I've been too busy to tell you about her."

"That girl who's always asking people to donate blood? The 'Blood Bank Cheerleader' is what they call her."

"Yeah, that's her," May replied with a sigh. "We'll be spending time with the donor as he hosts a fundraising event for the orphans so the kids can get some new clothes and other stuff they need."

"I might need to come along so I can get some new clothes, too!" Quin joked.

"Since we'll be busy with the setup, it's not bad that you'll be recovering during the break."

Quin felt a wave of relief knowing that spring break would no longer be an issue.

The problem now was his intensified concerns about their relationship. May just explained how his injury was convenient for her.

"I started looking for a job online!"

"Oh, that's nice. Maybe soon you won't be so broke that you're afraid to check your own bank account. You plan on working with that ankle?"

"That's funny. I'll get better soon and have the job ready to go by that time. And when I start working, I'll be able to get you a car before next year starts."

"Wow!" May replied. "I would really like that! It would be nice not having to hitch rides from others."

"Yeah, I know! I'll get one for you."

"You're the best, Quin!" May replied, as she leaned in to give him a hug. "I've already worked out assignments with my professors. I'll leave campus early to get the fundraiser and kids ready."

"You'll be super busy."

"Yeah, but I'll still check on you. I'm going to go for now. I have to finish some errands and then go to the hotel."

"The hotel?"

"Annalisa and I will have our own rooms at the hotel owned by the donor. Have you told your parents about your injury?"

"I'd rather be back in China and taking the Gaokao than to tell them."

"I really wish I could take care of you like the last time you were injured, but the timing is really bad right now."

"Forget about it, I got this covered," replied Quin with a thumbs up. "I'm not going to inconvenience you again."

As May picked up her belongings and left, Quin felt excited knowing his relationship with May had something to look forward to.

Quin would enjoy having his dorm room all to himself. There was a roommate, but he was already away visiting his family and wouldn't be back for a while. The solitude reminded Quin why he would not be spending time with his own family during the break.

He no longer had a family to visit.

There was little contact between Quin and May while she was tending to the orphans and her new donor. Quin wanted to give his girlfriend the space she needed. Video games passed the time for Quin until spring break was over.

Toward spring break's end, Quin looked forward to seeing May again. He sent messages to both her phone and social sites but received no response.

The next day he tried calling May but didn't get an answer.

Now worried, Quin assumed the worst—maybe May was kidnapped, had gotten hurt, or was in a car accident. He sent a few more concern-laced texts. While waiting for a response, he checked her social sites for recent posts. Nothing new.

From her site's photos, he found the name of the hotel where she was staying.

It was called "Ambit Inn." An internet search found that it was a four-star hotel with good ratings and beautiful photos.

"If I call this hotel, they most likely won't give me information about the guests, even if I claim to be the boyfriend. I want to go there, but I don't know her room number," Quin said aloud to himself.

His text message notification chimed. He quickly picked up his phone, hoping it was a message from May.

It was a message from May!

Quin unlocked his phone and read, "You can't take care of me."

Confused, he texted back, "What do you mean? Are you okay? I'm worried about you."

Not wanting to wait for a response and knowing her phone was in her hand, Quin called her. It went straight to voicemail.

He called again. It went straight to voicemail—again.

A third and final call. Still straight to voicemail.

Quin suspected May was in a bad service area. He checked her social platform again a little while later for updates—only to find she wasn't appearing in his traffic. He could not even find her account anywhere. Even searching her name yielded no results.

He had been blocked.

Not wanting to believe what was happening and stressed from trying to understand, Quin lay down and fell asleep.

When Quin awoke, there were no new messages on his phone.

There was nothing new on social media, and he was still unable to see May's profile. He theorized this was May's way of ending their relationship, but he was not prepared for that scenario. A face-to-face conversation was needed for answers, but first he needed to find out exactly where May was at the Ambit Inn.

Remembering that May mentioned being with Annalisa, Quin searched for the "Blood Bank Cheerleader's" account. Her nickname became obvious.

Annalisa's platform consisted heavily of blood donating material, followed by exercise videos and freelance modeling photos of herself. One of her most recent posts was an advertisement for a fundraising dinner that would include speeches, raffles, and a talent show performed by orphans. This had to be the same event May was preparing for. It was being held that night at 7 p.m. at the Ambit Inn.

Quin had to hurry since the current time was already 6 p.m.

After showering and putting on some fresh clothes, Quin noticed a small envelope at the foot of his dorm's door.

It was an invitation to the very event that Quin was preparing for. It read at the bottom: "Show at the ballroom's entrance."

Not wanting to waste time wondering who left the invitation, Quin slid the card into his pocket, grabbed his crutches, and departed to meet his ride to the hotel.

The Ambit Inn was so impressive that gazing at it made Quin forget why he was even there. After regaining his focus, he showed the invitation to the front desk, and they directed him to the ballroom where the fundraiser was being held.

When Quin reached the ballroom entrance, he met an individual that was clearly security.

"Good evening, good sir. May I see your invitation?"

Quin held up the card.

"Welcome sir! Enjoy the food and show. You can get a raffle ticket from the attendant inside, and she will assign you a table."

Quin entered the expansive ballroom. His reliance upon the crutches drew unwanted attention from the other guests while he searched for May.

Delicious-looking food, beautiful furniture, and lively chatter filled the room. Various security personnel were sprinkled around the borders of the room.

Once Quin spotted May, his heart sank in his chest. She was sitting next to and laughing with Annalisa.

To avoid unnecessary attention, Quin laid his crutches against a wall and discreetly limped his way toward May. Despite his attempt to remain discreet, eyes began to notice Quin.

When May looked his way and spotted him, she quickly stood up and walked to a nearby Caucasian man with an oddly shaped cane.

Grabbing him closely by the arm, May whispered in his ear. The man turned and looked at Quin.

The man waved at two security guards and pointed directly at Quin with his cane, prompting them to approach. Slightly shocked yet determined, Quin stayed put, intent on speaking with May despite the impending trouble.

When the two guards closed in, they each grabbed one of Quin's arms. Quin looked at May and the man with the cane as they watched Quin from the other end of the ballroom. With firm grips, they carried Quin out the ballroom.

"Put me down! What did I do?"

"The owner of this hotel wants you out," replied one of the guards.

Quin struggled to kick free, but his injured ankle throbbed painfully, stopping him. "I was invited! I have an invitation!"

"Welcome to private property," responded the other guard.

A third guard carrying Quin's crutches followed behind the two escorts carrying Quin.

Quin wasn't released until they placed him outside the hotel's doors.

"You are no longer welcome at this hotel. You are prohibited from returning. Have a nice day, sir."

Quin stood alone and embarrassed, crutches thrown to the ground next to him.

ASHLEY'S CHILDREN

Chapter 2: The Psychological Psychic

To humans, rejection is an undesirable experience.

Anyone who says otherwise is trying to fool you or themselves.

This is, at least, a strongly held belief for Quin High. This belief grew stronger when he realized acceptance is often celebrated while rejections give rise to negative emotions—emotions that are not to be shown.

Quin viewed rejection as avoidable with preparation. While some believe that rejection and being rejected provided lessons, Quin believed the lessons of rejection should never be preferred to the joys of acceptance.

This time, Quin was rejected by the woman he had a relationship with since high school, and he didn't even know the reason why.

His first suspicion was that it involved the man the hotel's security called "the owner." While Quin was being carried away, he noticed the owner's hand around May's shoulder. Quin concluded he must be the same owner May had mentioned a week ago in Quin's dorm room.

Back in his dorm room, Quin searched online to discover the owner's name.

"Roland Ambit."

Quin refused to believe May could leave him for anyone else and dismissed that possibility. He felt they loved each other, and that May would want to prevent being labeled a "leftover" by her family and peers. Quin also felt both of their parents would want them to be married as a sign that grandchildren would be assured. His upbringing stressed marrying young for the sake of that assurance. Quin's parents told him on various occasions that they could not die in peace unless they had grandchildren.

Seeing May with Roland forced Quin to ponder a thought he had never contemplated before—unlike him, May was not Chinese. Her mother was from Thailand, but her father was an American. Cultural differences might be an issue.

The next morning, as classes resumed after spring break, Quin chose to skip his classes due to recent events. He knew he'd be unable to focus even if he attended them.

He wanted to find a quiet spot outdoors to meditate. He found a small field and sat under a tree. With classes back in session, not many people were transiting the campus grounds. This was the perfect time and place to enjoy the fresh air alone.

After getting comfortable, Quin pondered what his parents would say if they knew about his current issues with May. Quin's parents never approved of her.

His focus broke when he sensed a presence approaching from behind. Quin turned around to see Annalisa looking down at him with the most heartwarming smile.

She was clearly Japanese. Her eyes possessed a welcoming and pleasant gaze that forced a smile across Quin's face. She smiled back and gently called his name.

"Quiiiiin."

At the sound of his name, Quin stood, smile still on his face. Just looking at Annalisa made his worries fade.

Annalisa hugged Quin, then took his hands in hers. "Let's get you inside and off that ankle. Follow me to the tea shop."

Without hesitation, Quin happily agreed.

Inside the tea shop, Annalisa seated Quin at a booth and ordered beverages. Upon returning, she sat directly across from Quin and smiled.

"Here, I got you your favorite—mango-flavored tea!"

"Thanks! How did you know my favorite flavor?"

"I learned a few things from May during the fundraiser."

The sound of May's name briefly brought worry back to Quin, and it showed on his face.

Annalisa's pleasant and delightful demeanor transitioned to a stern tone.

"I want to apologize for what happened to you yesterday at the fundraiser. It must've been stressful."

"It's something I'd like to forget. If my ankle wasn't messed up, it would have gone differently for those two guards."

"Absolutely!" she replied with her charm returning. "I've seen your fights. They weren't ready for your skills!"

This made Quin smile again. Then they both laughed and sipped their drinks.

"Quin, you've been free-style wrestling since middle school, right?"

"Yep! I love it! It's how I got accepted into Ward University!"

"I wrestled competitively before I transitioned to professional wrestling," said Annalisa.

"Ewww," Quin replied while laughing. "You stopped real wrestling to play that fake game?"

"The only thing fake about professional wrestling is the people who believe that it's fake."

They both laughed.

"When your ankle is better, I'll show you how fake my game is when I beat you!" Annalisa added.

More laughter came from them as they finished their drinks and continued chatting.

Quin was enjoying their time together. She made conversing easy and knew how to hold Quin's interest. The more they spoke, the better he felt.

Quin's problem now was wondering what May would say if she saw them having tea together like this. He figured Annalisa could answer a few questions he had about May.

"Annalisa, did May say anything else about me while you two were together?"

At this question, Annalisa's smile faded, as she reverted to the stern tone she displayed before.

"Be direct. Ask the real question you want answered," she replied with a heavy and mesmerizing stare. Quin paused for a few moments, contemplating her words.

"Is May cheating on me with Roland Ambit?"

"No," she calmly and confidently replied.

Quin smiled, relieved and happy to hear Annalisa's reassuring words. His hope to see his girlfriend again was restored. He no longer had to worry about how their parents would react. The plan to get a job and a car for May to reignite life into their relationship was again possible. Everything was going to be all right!

However, Annalisa's next words would change that.

"She's not cheating on you with Roland. She left you for Roland."

The next day when Quin awoke, he forced himself to prepare for class. He was determined to forget about May and move on.

I'm a skilled athlete, finding someone else will be easy. Anyone would want me, he thought.

When he opened the door to exit his dorm room, Annalisa stood on the other side.

She looked fantastic. Simple, yet fantastic.

"Hiii, Quiiin!"

Another smile spread across his face at the sound of her voice, as he unwillingly stared at her.

"Welll—are you going to invite me in or just keep staring?" she jokingly asked.

Quin quickly regained his senses to utter, "Sure! Come in! I'm glad you came by!"

Because of the bad news she delivered, Quin did not recall much from his time with Annalisa yesterday, but he did remember enjoying her company. He didn't mind missing class to spend more time with her, so he placed his bags and crutches down when she sat at his desk.

"I hope you're feeling better after yesterday's bad news," she said.

Quin sighed deeply in response—not wanting to relive the experience.

"In our cultures, we tend to solve our problems by ignoring them, but that won't help your situation," continued Annalisa. "I can see how traumatic this is for you. I would like us to spend more time together so you can feel better."

Quin remained silent, wondering why she would care, but the idea of spending more time with Annalisa made him ignore his question.

"Let's forget class today and visit a psychic I know. She offers the first few sessions for free. I can promise that after today, you will feel much better," Annalisa continued.

"That sounds fun. I'll only know she's real if she can explain why you choose fake wrestling over real matches."

"You're funny! When your ankle gets better, I'll show you while you're tapping out!"

Annalisa led Quin to her car. Quin left his crutches behind although his ankle still hurt. He was determined to enjoy Annalisa's company without inconveniences.

Quin liked being in Annalisa's vehicle. It was clean and gently filled with her perfume fragrance.

"Is this your parents' car?" Quin asked.

"No, it's mine," she replied.

"Where did you get it from? I'm looking—or was looking for a car."

Before Annalisa answered his question, Quin's stomach growled loudly.

"What did you eat today, Quin?"

"Nothing yet. I'll get something from the vending machine later."

"As loud as your stomach was, you'll need more than vending machine food. Let's eat together at my favorite restaurant after we see the psychic."

"Sure," Quin replied with false confidence. He knew he didn't have enough money to eat out, but he was too embarrassed to let Annalisa know that. He had to think of something before the end of the psychic session to prevent any shame.

"What else did May say about me while you two were fundraising?"

Annalisa glanced at Quin but remained silent, prompting him to repeat his question.

"Now is a good time for you to get out your comfort zone and start opening up to me. It will make our visit to the psychic better," she responded.

"What do you mean?"

"It's difficult in our cultures to discuss family problems with outsiders. Let's try changing that before we arrive."

Quin remained silent; he didn't have a response.

"Is it true you joined May's religion against your parent's wishes?" she asked.

Quin, wanting to please Annalisa, gathered the strength to say, "Yes."

"Were you baptized?"

"Yes."

Quin was thankful no more questions followed and felt uncomfortable after making such a confession to Annalisa.

As Annalisa continued driving, dark clouds filled the sky, and rain soon followed. The closer Quin and Annalisa came to the destination, the heavier the rain became.

Annalisa parked in front of a poorly lit one-story house with heavily boarded windows. The house seemed well-kept and abandoned at the same time. This made Quin suspicious, however, Annalisa seemed perfectly comfortable when she opened the front door without even bothering to knock!

Inside was a neatly kept house with minimal furniture and storage boxes scattered around. It was difficult to determine if the occupant was moving in or out.

Annalisa led Quin around a corner to a living room area. In the center of that room was a woman sitting at a small table.

Her white hair and black clothing reminded Quin of the Emo kids he attended middle school with.

Her eyes appeared to be pink. It was difficult to tell in the current lighting. There was very little light in the house.

"Quin, dear! So nice to meet you!"

She approached Quin with overwhelming confidence.

"Uhhh— hi," Quin replied, stunned by her forwardness and questionable British accent.

She hugged and kissed both of Quin's cheeks. Quin felt so uncomfortable that his stomach growled again.

She then led him to sit down at the table and seated herself next to him.

"My name is Ashley Akkadian."

Quin took several seconds of silence trying to figure out where Ashley was from. Ashley stared silently back with a grin that implied she knew what he was puzzled about.

Not wanting to appear rude, Quin finally responded, "I guess it was Annalisa who told you my name?"

Instantly, Ashley's demeaner transitioned to a more serious tone, and her smile faded. "I've known Ms. Usui for a long time. So long that, it'll be difficult to convince you I'm a medium; therefore, I won't try."

"That's a relief. I don't believe in psychics anyway."

"That doesn't mean we can't solve your problems. If you do as I say, after this day, I promise you will feel much better."

Quin was intrigued. He wanted to find out what gave her the confidence to make such a statement.

Ashley pointed to a table behind her with a small buffet of fruits and vegetables and asked, "Before we get started, would you like something to eat, dear?"

"No, thank you," Quin responded.

"I would have guessed differently by the sound of your stomach," Ashley joked with the return of her smile. "Annalisa, something to eat?"

"It depends on Quin," said Annalisa, shifting her attention to Quin. "We could save by eating here, or would you rather go out?"

Quin didn't like taking food from strangers, but in this moment, he knew that if they ate Ashley's food, he could avoid going to a restaurant and prevent Annalisa from discovering he was unable to afford eating out.

Quin agreed to eat Ashley's food. Ashley was happy about Quin's acceptance.

"Absolutely wonderful, dearest Quin! Eat all you can!"

While Quin and Annalisa were eating, Ashley placed a glowing, hand-sized, golden rock on the table and walked into the kitchen area. The glow from the rock was bright enough to illuminate the room like an uncovered lamp.

When Quin and Annalisa finished eating, Ashley returned and cleared the table except for the glowing rock.

She sat down across from Quin and smiled.

"You ate that food so fast; I take it you enjoyed it?"

"It was great," replied Quin, smiling at the knowledge that Annalisa would not yet find out he was low on cash.

"Lovely that you enjoyed it. Let's turn our attention to the reason you came here today. Although you've known me for a short time, we'll need you to step beyond your comfort zone and tell me what's troubling you."

"I'm embarrassed to say," Quin replied as he remembered Annalisa making the same statement during the drive to Ashley's house. Quin turned to look at Annalisa, but she was no longer in the room.

"I suppose it would only be fair that I tell you a little bit about myself first, right? How about I share a story with you, and then you share yours?"

"I guess. I just usually don't share family issues."

"Understandable. Personal rejections can be an emotional struggle that can cause long-term psychological damage."

"What? I—I didn't say anything about that."

Ashley pointed to the glowing rock on the table suggesting it informed her. She then picked the rock up and started speaking to it.

"The frozen past bears clothes woven for justice.

Ignore it or you will never find the defiant tower."

When Ashley finished speaking, she stared at the rock as if she were watching a video. Quin tried looking at the rock from different angles to see what she was viewing, but he could not see anything other than its light. She continued looking into it until it stopped glowing.

"I don't know how much Annalisa told you about me or how much she already knows," Quin said, believing Ashley's actions were staged.

"During separations, each partner will have a very different account of what happened. Anything May told Annalisa can't be considered for your recovery."

Quin took a deep breath. He did not know if he could believe Ashley's statements or not.

"I once had a sister," Ashley continued. "She and I were very close until a very special individual entered our lives. He was unlike anyone we'd ever met. My sister and I both fancied this gentleman and both of us wanted his hand in marriage. When he chose to marry me over my sister, my sister began to hate me."

Quin wanted to react to Ashley's story, but he didn't want to appear judgmental.

"Not only did the relationship between my sister and I become one filled with resentment, she also taught her children to hate me and my children as well. One of the last letters my sister wrote to me said, 'I will forever find peace in the grave knowing that my sister will forever live with a curse.'"

Quin frowned with surprise. "I thought I had it rough with my Chinese parents."

"Most young people think that until they get older."

"I suppose it's my turn to talk."

"I have a better idea," Ashely injected. "Tell me tomorrow."

"I'll be busy with classes tomorrow."

"I'm confident you'll find the time to return. You will feel more comfortable sharing once you've had a chance to form your thoughts. You and Annalisa should enjoy the rest of your day."

Quin felt relief when Ashley guided him out of the room. He was not prepared to share his story.

Ashley took Quin by the hand and led him to Annalisa, who was waiting in her car. After driving away, Annalisa made no mention of what had transpired at Ashley's house. She instead returned Quin to the campus and told him to think about where they should spend their time together tomorrow when his class was over.

The next morning, Quin spent most of the class thinking about May and Annalisa. Although only his third day of knowing Annalisa personally, he already found himself resisting feelings for her.

At the end of the class, Quin tried thinking of a place he and Annalisa could go to, but he didn't have the budget for anything. He wanted to hurry back to his dorm room to think of a plan in peace.

When the class ended, Quin was surprised to see that Annalisa was waiting for him outside the classroom door. He was excited to see her, but also afraid that she might find out he was broke.

"Quiiin! Did you decide on what you want to do today?"

"I honestly didn't. I had a lot on my mind."

"How about we visit Ashley again? You seem to be in better shape since you saw her yesterday. She'll have food again also."

Knowing that the session and food would be free, Quin agreed to return.

Near Ashley's house, the clouds were just as dark, and the rain was just as heavy as yesterday.

When Quin and Annalisa arrived, Ashley greeted them both and led Quin to the same table from the previous day. Food for Quin was already on the table.

After Quin finished eating, Ashley sat directly across from him and again spoke to the same glowing rock.

"The frozen past bears clothes woven for justice.

Ignore it or you will never find the defiant tower."

When Ashley finished speaking, the rock illuminated the entire room.

Able to see the entire room clearly now, Quin spotted a black and white picture hanging on the wall behind Ashley. He did not remember seeing it the previous day. It was a photo of a tall, well-built male. Determining his origins was difficult, but the individual looked impressive. Ashley stared at Quin as Quin stared at the photo.

"After today, you may meet him," she said in reference to the photo. "If you do, please let me know immediately."

"Sure, is that your husband?"

"No. However, he is very special to me, and I'm looking for him."

Quin looked around for Annalisa, but she was no longer in the room. When Quin looked back at Ashley, she was staring at the rock.

"Is that a voice activated lamp? It doesn't have a cord or battery slot," Quin said.

"It's called the Author's Ending. It's my version of a crystal ball that gives me a limited view of someone's future."

Quin looked at the rock again but still could not see anything.

"I know you don't believe me right now, so we can start with you sharing your story of what's troubling you. Annalisa cannot hear us; there is no reason to be ashamed."

Quin stood and looked outside the room for Annalisa. When he could not see her anywhere, he sat back down.

"I'm the first son in my family. My parents brought me to the United States when I was very young. They did not want me dating until I finished college and wanted me to be with a Chinese woman when I did marry. They were very upset when I started a relationship with May during high school. May isn't Chinese."

Ashley gave Quin her full attention and remained quiet while he spoke.

"My grades were good in high school but not the best. Because my parents think like we're still in China and must prepare for the Gaokao, they often panicked about me not having the best grades. They would sometimes consider me a failure and blamed it on my relationship with May."

Quin paused to take a breath and to see if Ashley was following his story. She continued to remain silent.

"After I converted to May's religion, my parents no longer wanted anything to do with me. They made me choose between them or her. I chose to use my scholarship to attend Ward University with May so we could be together, but she just left me for another guy and I'm not sure why. I just lost everyone in my life, and now I don't know what to do. To make it all worse, I'm low on cash and the guy she left me for probably does have money."

Ashley didn't respond until several seconds after Quin finished speaking.

"I would also feel terrible if the lover I sacrificed my family for left me for someone else."

Quin bowed his head in shame.

"Because mate opportunities are typically rare and difficult to obtain, it is becoming common for friends and family members to betray each other for a potential partner."

Quin, head still bowed, mumbled back to Ashley, "I wish I could go back in time."

"Quin, dear," Ashley continued with an intruding glare. "I have just one question to ask before I give you a very special present."

"Yes?"

"When you switched to Christianity for May, were you properly baptized?"

"I didn't mention what religion, but yes, I was," Quin replied with a curious tone.

Before Ashley stepped out of the room, she smiled and pointed at the Author's Ending, suggesting it revealed the minor detail.

When Ashley returned, she handed Quin a brown bag and told him what was inside would solve his problems.

Quin looked inside to see that it was a flat, skull-like mask with a somewhat theatrical design. Quin wanted to question how a mask would help, but he didn't want to seem ungrateful.

"Wait until nightfall before wearing it. Don't try it on while the sun is up, or it won't work," Ashley said with a smile.

Ashley led Quin outside to Annalisa and her car. After driving away, Annalisa didn't question Quin about what he spoke to Ashley about. She instead surprised Quin with one of his favorite take-out dishes, a large order of grilled salmon and broccoli.

When Annalisa returned Quin to his dorm, she placed the mask on his desk and hugged him goodbye. After she left, Quin ate his food and fell asleep.

ASHLEY'S CHILDREN

Chapter 3: The Mask

Quin awoke later in the evening feeling refreshed.

There were no new phone notifications, and he was still blocked by May.

The mask Ashley gave him earlier that day lay on the nearby desk. Quin removed the wrappings to further examine it. The mask felt different from other masks. It was not made of flexible plastic or rubber as a regular costume mask would be. It was very sturdy and felt tougher than bone.

With nothing to lose and in accordance with Ashley's instructions, Quin put on the mask.

The mask instantly latched itself onto Quin's face.

Pain spread through Quin's body as the mask sapped his energy. A severe thirst filled his throat as his vision faded. He tried taking the mask off, but its grip was too strong. After several seconds of struggling, Quin's eyesight went dark.

When's Quin's vision returned, he found himself standing in the parking lot outside his dorm room. His severe thirst was gone and nearby were two motionless bodies.

Looking at the bodies, he recognized them as two free spirits, who lived nearby and collected bottles from trash cans as their source of income.

Quin looked around trying to piece together what happened, and why he was outside. No one was around.

Quin fled from the bodies before anyone got the chance to witness him nearby.

After escaping from the scene to a building a few blocks away, Quin looked down at his injured ankle. It no longer hurt.

He removed the CAM boot to examine his ankle more closely. It felt better than ever.

To test that all the pain was gone, Quin began hopping up and down. He continued jumping in astonishment at how much height he could now reach.

While determining whether this was a dream, Quin remembered placing the mask he put on his face. It was still on his face. Quin resumed jumping up and down, amazed at how long he could remain in the air before touching the ground. He was reaching at least ten feet.

"More—" the masked whispered. "Get more—"

Quin felt thirsty again. Thoughts of blood dominated his mind.

Although Quin wanted to return to the dorm, he walked in the opposite direction. The mask was guiding him somewhere.

Walking a short distance away, Quin spotted another free spirit sleeping on the ground behind a secluded building.

After rationalizing that no one would miss him, Quin lifted the man with a single hand and bit into the vagrant's neck.

The vagrant screamed, but Quin ignored it and kept drinking.

I'm not myself! I'm sucking the blood out of this guy! I need this! I need this so much!

Quin did not let go of the victim until his thirst was quenched. After Quin dropped the individual, he felt new elongated canine fangs in his mouth.

This must have been what I did to those other two I saw on the ground earlier. I need to get back and hide now!

Quin rushed back to his dorm. While running, he noticed he covered more distance than usual without tiring. He was much faster than before.

This isn't real, Quin thought.

While running back to his dorm, he felt terrible for the three people he just harmed, but also felt justified since his cravings were so strong.

Quin successfully returned to his dorm room unnoticed. Inside his room, Quin was too confused to properly process all the recent events.

This mask has done something to me; must take it off!

With a firm tug, Quin removed the mask from his face.

He felt normal again.

Without having time to question the events, Quin passed out from exhaustion.

When the morning sunlight woke Quin up the next morning, the mask was lying nearby on the floor.

His memories felt like a dream, but various bloodstains and his healed ankle convinced him it was all real.

After staring at it for several moments, Quin placed the mask on his face again.

Instantly, an intense heat engulfed his face. The heat was coming from the morning sunlight entering through his window. It was like standing pointblank at a fireplace.

Quin quickly snatched the mask off to escape the torture. Ashley's instructions to wear it at night now made sense. Full of questions, Quin called Annalisa but got no answer, and her voicemail was full.

After sending her a text message, Quin noticed he was starving as if he had not eaten anything for days. He ate nearly all the food he could find in his room. Afterwards, he made another call to Annalisa. Still no answer.

With Quin's ankle now better, searching the campus grounds for Annalisa on foot was his next goal. He also wanted to use this opportunity to look for May.

After searching the entire campus, Quin could not find either of them anywhere. There was nothing new on Annalisa's social platform and Quin assumed May was still staying at the Ambit Inn.

Quin wanted to call Ashley, but he did not have her number. There were no internet search results for her contact information. He decided to return to her house.

At Ashley's house, the signs of life from the past two days were completely gone. No response came from knocking at the door, and nothing could be seen through the boarded windows. Also, the door was locked.

Determined to get answers, Quin removed one of the window's boards and entered through it. There was still no response when he called out Ashley's name from inside the house.

The house lay empty, shrouded in darkness with all the lights unresponsive. Quin's cell phone flashlight was the only way to see. The few decorations and boxes from yesterday had been removed except the picture of the impressive looking individual on the wall.

Quin looked at his mask and remembered the burning torture he experienced in his dorm room. He concluded the windows of the house were boarded to keep out sunlight.

Ashley must have a mask like this, and Annalisa knows something, too!

Wanting to test his theory, Quin closed the curtain on the window he entered through and placed on his mask. The familiar pain from last night returned along with the thirst— forcing him to his knees.

Despite the agonizing pain, Quin could smell what he was craving through the torture.

Blood.

It smelled delicious and was nearby.

The scent led him to a room at the back of the house with a locked chest. Quin easily broke the lock off the chest with his bare hand. Inside the chest were several packets containing blood.

Unable to think past his thirst, he drank from the packets until the pain and thirst subsided.

With his rational thinking restored, Quin observed how he was able to see perfectly well in the dark and could even read!

Looking at the now empty blood packets, he noticed they bore the same name promoted on Annalisa's social media page, "Blood Bank of Ward." This confirmed his theory that Ashley and Annalisa must both have masks like his.

Looking for more clues, Quin searched all the rooms, including the room with the photo on the wall.

Quin stared at the photo again, trying to determine the race of the individual in the picture.

As he looked at the photo, his eyes fixed themselves on the picture. He was unable to look away or move his entire body.

Time seemed to stand still as his vision steadily blurred to black. As the blur intensified, the words formed in the middle of the darkness:

"THE ANGEL THAT SHINES"

After several seconds, the letters and darkness slowly dispersed like a cloud, allowing Quin to see and move again.

With his senses restored, Quin found himself kneeling in front of the photo and breathing hard.

Overwhelmed with fear, Quin removed the mask from his face and fled from Ashley's house in haste.

ASHLEY'S CHILDREN

Chapter 4: Quin vs. Roland

When Quin returned to his dorm room, there was an unfamiliar box on his desk.

Inside the box were two 32 oz. flasks. They both contained foul-smelling blood. Attached was a sticky note that read: "Drink this instead of people's blood."

Knowing Annalisa must have placed the box in his room, Quin called her but received no answer.

How did she get inside my room without a key, especially since my roommate hasn't yet returned?

Also inside the box was an address written on a card with a floor number. An internet search showed the location as "Ambit Services," a company owned by Roland Ambit.

Unsure why Annalisa would reveal Roland's location to him, Quin saw it as an opportunity to get payback against Roland for stealing May. Excited at the prospect, Quin looked forward to wearing the mask again and confronting Roland that night.

Quin was reluctant to seek revenge, but he believed his unique situation deserved vengeance, given it involved the woman he hoped to marry.

When night came, Quin put on the mask. The similar pain and thirst from before returned, but his attention was taken by the smell of the blood-filled flasks in the box. They now smelled wonderful compared to before.

He poured the contents of one flask into his mouth. It was the most delicious beverage he'd ever tasted.

After drinking the flask dry, the pain subsided along with his thirst. The beverage made him feel energized and invincible.

Fueled by adrenaline, Quin was eager to confront Roland.

Quin arrived at the Ambit address. It was a tall building surrounded by a wide parking lot decorated with trees.

From the edge of the parking lot, Quin scanned the building and noticed a balcony with the lights on. The balcony appeared to be on the same floor written on the card.

Quin climbed and jumped up the building's wall to reach the balcony. When Quin entered the balcony, he saw a workspace office with a single desk in the middle and various art works, trophies, and awards along the walls.

Behind the center of the desk stood Roland Ambit. He was tall and very well poised. Despite Quin's appearance with his mask, Roland appeared perfectly calm and even welcoming when he spotted Quin.

Should I knock him out? Drink his blood? Just scare him into leaving May alone? Maybe breaking everything in this room will be enough, Quin pondered.

Roland continued looking directly at Quin, both hands placed on the same cane he had at the hotel. Seeing Roland holding a cane actually made Quin feel guilty about thinking of doing any harm at all to this man.

"We've yet to be properly introduced," Roland said with an obviously British accent. "I'm Roland Ambit. May I ask who you are?"

Quin said nothing in response.

"If I'd known we'd be having guest tonight, I would have had my guards prepare some tea for us. What has led you to my office tonight?"

Without hesitation, Quin shouted, his voice tense, "I want you to leave May alone!"

"Then you must be Mr. High. Young May has told me a lot about you."

"Don't speak her name!" Quin angrily shouted.

"Try composing yourself, Quin. It doesn't seem you planned tonight well. What did you hope to achieve by coming here?"

"I plan to get her back, and I'll hurt you if I need to!"

A smile formed on Roland's face as he calmly replied, "Women despise pursuit by men they lack interest in."

Angered by his words, Quin lunged through the air at Roland.

To Quin's surprise, he was knocked back with a sudden swing of Roland's cane and fell to the ground.

Ignoring the strength that had pushed him back, Quin quickly got up and lunged again, only to be met with precise strikes from Roland's cane.

Each hit from the cane sent electric shocks through Quin's body, akin to being tasered. The strikes continued, sending jolts of electricity through his body, forcing him to take steps back.

The strikes persisted, pushing Quin further back until he fell off the balcony and crashed into a parkedcar below.

Quin was hurt, but he felt himself recovering swiftly from the pain. After a few moments, he climbed out of the now destroyed car and looked up toward the balcony to see Roland looking down. Considering the distance, Quin couldn't believe that he survived the fall.

Can I avoid being killed by wearing this mask?

Quin's questions were interrupted by the sudden appearance of uniformed men, each armed with taser wands.

They wore black combat clothes with grey reflective vests and ski masks. Their faces couldn't be identified. Only their eyes could be seen through their ski masks.

The masked men moved quickly to surround Quin, drew their taser wands, and began shouting various threats at Quin.

"This fight will take a lot of effort and backbone, two things you don't have!"

"There comes a time in a man's life when he must surrender! Your time is now!"

"You can't read, you can't write, and you can't win this fight!"

Driven by instinct, Quin turned and fled towards his dorm. While Quin fled, he could hear one of the masked men ask, "Is insurance going to cover these damages to my car?"

The next morning, Quin reflected on what had happened the previous night.

A middle-aged man with a cane beat a college athlete.

That alone was enough for Quin to prepare for another encounter that night! Except this time he would need plan of attack.

Taking that cane from Roland would leave him defenseless, Quin thought. *It's some kind of technological weapon. When he swings it at me, I'll grab it, snatch it, and then break it in half! Then I'll drink his blood! Not all of it—just enough to hospitalize him until I get May back.*

That night, placing the mask on was less painful than before. Quin drank from the other flask inside the box, satisfying his thirst and giving him another burst of energy.

After jumping out his window, Quin took a moment to observe the campus and buildings around him.

With the mask on, the city lay open before him, no area seemed out of reach. He was able to run up walls, hop from one building top to another, and lift heavy objects. With these abilities, there was nothing he couldn't achieve.

Making his way into the city area, Quin stood atop one of the tallest buildings and observed the beautiful sight of Ward City, home to Ward University. Gazing at the fancy hotels and beautiful cars began to inspire Quin to want more out of life.

With the mask's power, achieving almost anything would be easy. He could work in construction, become an undefeated professional fighter, offer his services to the military. The possibilities with the mask were limitless.

With the money and fame, Quin could reignite his plans to gain social status and provide for May. Except with the mask, it would be done on a much grander and more impressive scale. Getting married to May would be possible again, and when they had children, Quin's parents would accept him back.

"Is this what Ashley meant when she said this mask would solve my problems?" Quin asked out loud.

Maybe, but Roland must be out of the way first, he answered to himself.

Roland's building was the same as yesterday with one exception. The same uniformed guards that caused Quin to run away the night before were now patrolling the parking lot. They seemed prepared for another encounter.

Taking out the guards one by one along the way to prevent any possible interference was an option, but Quin decided against it. He wanted to end this quickly and without notice. Using the shadows and parked cars for cover, Quin quietly navigated through the parking lot and up the building walls to the same balcony as before.

Although the lights were on in the office, no one was inside. A strong stench of garlic could be smelled from the ceiling. The smell was so foul, Quin turned around to leave.

Before he departed, something caught his eye.

Near the office desk rested the cane Roland used as a weapon the night before.

Quin wanted to understand his defeat the night before. He covered his nose and held his breath to navigate through the terrible odor of garlic. He planned to quickly grab the cane and leave with it.

When Quin approached the walking stick, a cloud of powder fell upon him. It was a cloud of garlic powder. That cloud made his skin itch and his body feel heavy.

Realizing he was in trouble, Quin started moving back to the balcony to escape the cloud, but his legs were slow in responding.

This was planned! They set a trap!

To confirm his conclusion, two uniformed guards entered through the office door wielding taser wands. They rushed to Quin and immediately began striking him with their weapons.

"Have you ever been under citizen's arrest before?" asked one of the guards.

Quin fell to the ground, still unable to move. The guards continued their assault. Stunning and painful jolts of electricity coursed through Quin's body.

"Is this the end?" Quin muttered as his vision began to fade.

Before blacking out Quin heard one of the guards say, "Like a house infested with termites, your plans for tonight have collapsed!"

When Quin awoke, he found himself in a place he never wished to be.

A jail cell.

He sat up to see foul-smelling inmates crying while others were yelling at passing law enforcement officers.

What scared Quin the most was that the mask was no longer on his face. Without the mask, he was normal again and powerless.

He looked around the cell in a panic, realizing it was nowhere to be found.

ASHLEY'S CHILDREN

Chapter 5: Unexpected Parole

Inside the jail cell, Quin didn't know what was worse—the smell or the shame of anyone finding out he was in police custody.

Quin checked his pockets only to discover that his phone was also missing. He pondered who to call with his single phone call. May, his only real contact, had blocked him. Even if she hadn't blocked him, he didn't memorize her number since it was stored in his cell phone.

No contacts. No cell phone. No mask.

Behind bars, Quin was obsessed with the location of his mask. With it, escaping the cell would be a simple task. Legal matters could be evaded, and escaping to another city would be easy. Quin just had to find out where it was.

Ideally, he would ask the police officers, but getting their attention proved difficult.

I could start banging loudly on the bars, but the other inmates are already doing that, and it isn't working for them. I need another plan. I could fake a heart attack or seizure. That might allow me to talk to one of them. This place is like a zoo, and I'm on display! This would have gone differently if I used the mask to see May first!

As Quin fell deeper into thought, an officer approached and opened his cell.

"Quin High," the officer called, motioning for Quin to follow him.

Without a second thought, Quin eagerly exited his cell and followed the officer to the police station's outside entrance.

"You're free to go."

"Just like that?" Quin questioned.

"Yep. And there is your ride," said the officer, as he pointed toward the street.

Quin turned to see a black stretch limousine. A door was held open by a well-dressed chauffeur.

"I don't know who that is," Quin said to the officer, gesturing at the chauffeur.

"Your cell phone and Halloween mask are inside," the officer responded.

Assuming the officer meant his mask, Quin rushed inside the vehicle and searched for it.

Quin found the limousine's layout confusing, with seats aligned along the sides instead of in rows. A wall divided the driver's seat from the back seats. The ceiling was higher than normal with a sunroof in the center. The lights were very dim, making it difficult to see the back end of the vehicle.

Quin looked for a light switch, hoping it would reveal his mask.

Quin's concentration was broken at the sound of his name being called from the back of the limousine.

"Mr. High, welcome to my limousine."

Quin turned toward the voice, but the darkness obscured his view. When the lights came on, who Quin saw made his heart hollow.

It was Roland Ambit.

Quin stared intensely at Roland, who stared back. Quin's mind raced so quickly that a few seconds felt like several minutes.

As the staring continued, a flood of resentment filled Quin's hollow heart. There were many things Quin wanted to say, but the presence of Roland's cane kept him silent.

Eyes still locked on Quin, Roland slowly reached inside his jacket's front pocket and pulled out Quin's mask.

Quin felt a wave of relief seeing his mask again; however, worry soon followed seeing it in Roland's hand. Quin grew worried of what would happen if Roland wore the mask. He wanted to snatch it from Roland, but the painful memories of the cane made him fearful of getting close to Roland.

If he touches me with that cane, it will shock me! I don't know if I can survive a hit from it maskless.

When Quin looked at the vehicle's door as an escape route, he realized it was closed, and the car was already in motion. Searching for the mask had made him oblivious to his surroundings.

Holding up Quin's mask, Roland asked, "Does this belong to you, young man?"

"Yes, and it's very dangerous," Quin replied.

"How so?" Roland questioned.

"If you give it back, it can't hurt you."

"In due time. For now, let's have a conversation absent of breaking and entering."

Roland tucked the mask back into his jacket's pocket.

"We were introduced under unpleasant conditions. I would like us to start over with some good news. I was able to have your criminal charges dropped."

"I didn't hear of any charges."

"It's moot at this point. After you've gotten some rest, I would like to discuss how grateful my company would be to have you become a part of it."

"You—you want me to work for you?"

"Your talents can make you a very successful individual."

"Sorry, I've got school."

"No schooling can provide the special skills you displayed at my office."

Quin wanted to mention that he needed the mask to use those abilities, but he remained silent to avoid tempting Roland into wearing it.

"Considering your recent and tragic experiences, some recovery time would help clear your mind. It should help to know that your time in police custody will not be public."

"My parents won't find out?"

"No, they will not."

Quin felt a wave of relief knowing that his confinement would remain a secret. A small smile even formed on his face, but getting his mask back from Roland was still his top priority.

"Where are you taking me?"

"I have a room ready for you at one of my motels."

"I would prefer my dorm."

"I see. How about we take a mere look at the room I have prepared? If you don't like it, we can return you to the dorms."

"The police said you have my phone."

"It's inside the motel room."

Quin realized he was being pressured by Roland, however he felt complying was necessary to retrieve his mask.

The motel they arrived at was basic in appearance compared to the Ambit Inn. It consisted of only two floors and very few decorations.

Quin followed Roland to a second-floor room where he was given the room's key card. Inside the room, Quin saw everything he craved: food, water, a shower room, and a bed.

"You can use the room's phone to call the front desk for a free ride to your dorm," said Roland. "Your mobile device and a change of clothes are on the bed."

Quin grabbed his cell phone and checked it for notifications. The clothes lying on the bed seemed to be his correct size. Quin tried asking Roland where the garments came from, but he was gone. Quin looked outside the room to see Roland's limo driving away from the parking lot below.

Realizing that it was past 2 a.m. and his growing hunger, Quin went back into the room to shower, eat, and sleep.

As Quin fell deeper into sleep, a disturbing thought crossed his mind.

Roland now has two things important to me—my girlfriend and my mask.

ASHLEY'S CHILDREN

Chapter 6: The Second Mask

When Quin awoke, it was past noon.

Out of habit, and hope, Quin checked his social media to see if May's account was visible.

He was still blocked.

He tried calling Annalisa again. Still no answer.

Quin was torn between wanting to attend his classes and wanting to stay at the motel with the hope that Roland would return with his mask.

While he lay in bed contemplating, the motel's phone began ringing. Assuming it was Roland calling, he answered it.

"Hello?"

"Mr. High, I was confident you would choose my motel to hang your hat. The front desk can deliver food to your room free of charge."

"How did you know my clothes size and to get this room ready?"

"You'll have to pardon me. We have limited time. This mask of yours is a very intriguing object. Where did you get it from?"

Quin's heart skipped a beat wondering if Roland put the mask on. If he did, there was no way he would return it.

"A friend gave it to me as a gift."

"Interesting. Moving on, today I'd like to introduce you to the man that expedited your release last night. Afterwards, we can discuss a new opportunity for you and the return of your mask."

"All right. Inside my closet, I also found a suit in my size."

"Appropriate attire for the occasion. Please have it on by 3 p.m., and a driver will bring you to the meeting place."

"Where exactly are we meeting?"

Without receiving an answer, Quin heard the phone hang up.

By 3 p.m., Quin was dressed and ready to go. Another chauffeur, dressed more casually with a more standard car, retrieved Quin from the motel. Quin asked the driver where they were going, but he refused to answer.

While it bothered Quin not to know where he was being taken, the thought of receiving his mask back excited him enough not to worry.

I'll get my mask back, put it on, and run off as fast as I can!

The destination puzzled Quin. It was a church—a very large church. It could have been mistaken for a college campus.

There were many people gathering at this church—all dressed appropriately for the occasion. Local news station personnel were present as well.

A sign stated that a wedding for Jason Ward, the mayor of Ward City, was scheduled for today.

The driver drove Quin to a drop off zone and told Quin to wait. Before Quin could ask what he was waiting for, a hand landed on his shoulder.

It was Roland.

"I'm delighted you made it, Quin. Please follow me. We have much to discuss."

Roland led Quin through the crowds to a conference room. As Quin followed, he couldn't ignore that Roland was moving rather quickly for someone with a cane. It was as if he really didn't need it at all.

After they both took seats, Roland addressed Quin.

"As you have likely figured out, there is a wedding today. The mayor of this city, Jason Ward, is getting married. I did not inform you of the destination to prevent you from dwelling on your own situation before arriving. I knew you had aspirations of marrying young May."

Quin took a quiet and deep breath of frustration from Roland's words. Roland seemed to have noticed.

"While this is a difficult topic for you, it is something you and I must discuss if we are to ever become the friends I know that we can be."

Quin wanted to get up and leave the room, but he knew he couldn't just yet.

"While we cannot go into details now, know that May will not return to you. Instead of focusing your attention on her, redirect it for a future partner. To prevent easily losing your future partner to another, you must first become financially successful. Today you have an opportunity to begin pursuing the success you need."

Roland pulled out an envelope from his front pocket and handed it to Quin.

What Quin saw inside made him smile.

It was a check for $1,000.

"That is half of the total compensation you will receive for helping to protect tonight's wedding reception," Roland continued.

"Wow, this is only half? That's a lot! What am I protecting it from?"

"I'll explain later. For now, it's time to meet the man who ensured your release from detainment."

When Roland finished speaking, the room's door opened. A sharply dressed man walked in. He was tall with a head full of curly hair. His shaven face exposed a youthful appearance with Jewish features.

"Mayor Ward, this is Quin High. He will be replacing Danton tonight," said Roland.

"Excellent!" the mayor said, turning to Quin for a handshake.

"Jason Ward. Nice to meet you, Quin."

"Hello, Mayor, sir. Nice to meet you, sir."

"Please, call me Jason. I hear you attend Ward University. My brother is the president of that university. I hope he's treating you well there."

Quin, still excited from receiving the money replied, "Yes, sir!"

"I believe you and I will become great friends in the future! I wish we could talk more, but I've got to tie the knot for the second time. I'll see you two again soon."

After Jason briskly walked out of the room, Roland turned his attention back to Quin.

"We will have to continue our important conversation another time. For now, you should secure your compensation in a safe place and prepare for tonight."

"Sure, but I've still got my classes. I can't fail them."

"I'll talk to Mayor Ward's brother to help with that. The driver who brought you here will take you anywhere you need to go. Return by sunset to receive your mask back."

Quin went to his dorm room to change his clothes. Afterwards, he deposited the check he received into his bank account and purchased some of his favorite foods. He could now afford to eat out!

This was the first time in a long time that Quin had disposable income. He felt good.

When Quin's driver reminded him that it was time to return to the wedding, Quin got excited about receiving his mask back. A broad smile remained on his face for the entire drive back to the wedding.

When they arrived, the driver spoke on his cell phone and then handed it to Quin.

"It's Roland. He would like to speak to you."

Quin grabbed the phone.

"Roland, how do you afford all this stuff? The drivers and guards?"

"Are you majoring in journalism? This is no time for an interview. The driver will take you to the back of the church to meet my Ambit Guards. Eat the vitamin bar the driver gives you. It will reduce your urge to drink the blood of the party guests and my guards you'll be working with. Beware, it does not taste pleasant."

"How do you know about the mask? Did you put it on?"

"You are not the first person I've met with a mask like that, and you may meet one of them yourself tonight."

Not even 24 hours had passed since Quin had lost his mask; however, his desperation to reunite with it made it feel like a week.

Quin ate the vitamin bar given to him by the driver. It tasted horrible just as Roland warned. Quin followed the driver to the back of the church where they met with two Ambit Guards who presented Quin with his mask.

Quin was so overwhelmed with joy that he failed to realize that the two men returning his mask to him were dressed identically to the uniformed men from Roland's office.

Quin placed the mask on his face. Empowerment, confidence and nostalgia permeated Quin's entire body.

"*I missed you! I've missed you too! Getting May back! Getting married! Having children! Reuniting with my family! Income to make them forgive me! It is all possible again with you!*"

"Sorry, sir. Were you talking to us or on the phone?"

"Hmm? What?" Quin looked at the guards again and remembered where he saw their uniforms. "Aren't you the two that attacked me last night?"

"No, sir," responded one of the guards. "Those guards are off tonight."

Quin stared at the two guards while the driver returned to his vehicle. It was difficult to tell them apart and Quin couldn't smell the blood of either of them.

"That horrible tasting vitamin bar that was given to me, why was it so bad?"

"The raw and unique ingredients cause your body to produce more blood, which is then consumed by your mask. It lowers your urge to drink another human's blood, but you'll still need to drink blood soon before it wears off. We have some in the van for you."

"I want to know how you two know about this mask."

The two guards looked at each other for a moment before turning their attention back to Quin.

"Roland has an enemy that uses a mask like yours."

"That's how they knew to stun me in his office?"

"Exactly, sir."

"You guys don't have to call me 'sir.' You both seem older than me."

"All right, Quin-san."

"I'm Chinese, not Japanese."

"When you're ready, there are blood canisters located in the van, Quin-san."

Not being bothered by the title of "San," Quin spotted the van some yards away.

"Also, inside you'll find a letter from Roland," added one of the Ambit Guards.

Quin approached the van and found the letter. It was handwritten and read, "Do not change your fighting style to conform to the mask; let the mask enhance your pre-existing skills."

Confused, Quin asked the guards what it meant.

"He's saying to only use wrestling techniques while wearing your mask. During your fight in his office, you tried using acrobatic attacks without any experience."

A cloud of shame hovered over Quin knowing that the Ambit Guards knew about his loss to Roland.

"You two know a lot. What are your names?"

The two looked at each other for a moment before turning back to Quin.

"We know the name of Roland's enemy. It's 'Earnest.'"

"He has rodent facial features and doesn't shower often. If you miss his face, you can't miss his odor."

"He and I won't get along then. Showers are a must for me," Quin replied.

"To prevent the wedding guests from seeing your face, it might be best to stay on the rooftops."

"Yeah, I need some time alone anyway."

"Please be careful not to let anyone see you with your mask on, Quin-san."

"I'm still not Japanese."

Quin drank a canister of blood and climbed his way to the roof.

On the roof, Quin was so happy, he felt like jumping from rooftop to rooftop, but instead, he chose to sit and meditate.

I finally got you back! I never want to take you off again! Now I can get May back! At first, I wanted to beat Roland to get her back, but Roland is much nicer than I thought and is now paying me. This means I'll need a new plan. I could talk to him about giving May back to me. He said she would never return to me, but I can't just accept that. If he is not willing to give her back to me, I need a backup plan. I could start attending Church again to get her attention since she's a religious woman. But which church? They all claim to follow the same book, but have different beliefs. They all can't be correct. Even if I knew, she said I couldn't take care of her. Maybe first I should—what is that terrible smell?

Quin could hear his name being called from the same direction as the odor, "Quin-san!"

Quin hurried to the rooftop closest to the guard's location and the odor.

The source of the odor fit the description given to Quin earlier by the guards. He wore a white mask and his rodent-like facial features were more apparent than Quin imagined.

Earnest's clumsy and unathletic posture contradicted the impression Quin had developed from hearing about an enemy of Roland. He expected someone more intimidating.

Quin wanted to observe more, but seeing Earnest shove the two guards aside to make his way to the van containing the blood prompted Quin to attack.

Quin jumped off the roof and tackled Earnest into the ground. Earnest fell much more easily than Quin had anticipated.

"Oops," Earnest said, looking up at Quin.

Earnest stood and threw a sloppy punch, which Quin easily ducked before throwing Earnest back to the ground.

"I'm sorry! I won't do it again, Draft Dodging Danny," Earnest said with a regretful tone.

Wanting to get a better look at his mask, Quin lifted Earnest up by the neck and held him in place.

Earnest tried to break Quin's grip but was unsuccessful. Quin prepared to question Earnest, but the two Ambit Guards arrived and assaulted Earnest with their taser wands.

The guards attacked Earnest from both sides, forcing him to the ground and into the fetal position.

Quin stepped back to watch. He was happy that the guards were fighting on his side this time.

"I give up! Sorry about that. It'll never happen again. I didn't know you had another mask, Draft Dodging Danny!"

Earnest then scurried away from the guards' onslaught, disappearing into the thick of some nearby trees and bushes.

Quin and the two guards stared intently until they were sure Earnest was completely gone.

"Nice slam, Quin-san!"

When Quin questioned the guards about Earnest, they said Roland would have more information and that they were missing details.

When the wedding was over, the guards returned Quin to his motel room in their van.

When Quin awoke the next afternoon, he found another check for $1,000 at the foot of his door. He couldn't wait to deposit it.

However, after recapping the events of last night, he had many questions and wanted answers. A call to Roland was the first step.

"Mr. High, excellent work last night on your victory over Earnest."

"Thanks. It was easier than I expected. Know where he got that mask from?"

"Perhaps the same place you received yours? You did not provide details on that subject."

Quin did not want to mention Ashley to Roland, so he changed the subject.

"Is there any way we can talk today?"

"Why, yes. I'll send a driver to bring you to my location where you'll receive another advance."

Excitement filled Quin's voice as he asked, "Another advance? For another job?"

"The skills you displayed last night are very valuable and are needed again tonight. I'll brief you when you arrive."

Quin was delighted to learn that the meeting location was at the beach. Everything was beautiful and captivating up and down the sandy lanes. The sunshine and temperature were both perfect. The beach was empty except for the security detail scattered about.

Despite knowing he could not use it during the day, Quin still brought his mask along with him. He feared losing it again if he left it inside the motel room. Before arriving at the beach, Quin purchased a sling backpack to store and carry the mask.

Upon arrival, Roland was already waiting for Quin at the scene.

"It is a pleasure to see you again, Quin. Welcome to Mayor Ward's honeymoon beach house. Please follow me to the guest house."

The inside of the guest house was pleasant. It was a two-bedroom house complete with a full kitchen and living room.

"Let's sit at the table, shall we? Feel free to enjoy the tea and cookies."

"No thanks, not hungry."

"I am thankful we can converse today. I know that by the end of our conversation many barriers to our friendship will be removed."

"Possibly."

"Before we begin, I wanted to give you this. It is a token of appreciation from Mayor Ward for your positive performance last night."

Roland handed Quin an envelope containing $300. A smile crossed Quin's face.

"And here is half of the compensation for tonight."

Roland handed Quin another check for $1,000. Quin's smile grew uncontrollably wider.

"I'm glad to see you're happy," Roland continued. "After tonight you will receive the remainder."

"Yes—I think we can become good friends," Quin responded. They both laughed.

"I'm sure you have many questions. I hope we can get around to most of them."

"I have too many."

"Let's begin with last night's triumph."

"Who was that guy? Do you know him?"

"Earnest is a bad egg who sought to steal a very special crystal from Mayor Ward last night. Thanks to your efforts, he was unsuccessful."

"I thought mayors controlled the police. They could have stopped the theft since you or they knew about it."

"While Earnest isn't competent with his abilities, he still easily outmatches a normal person with standard weaponry, such as the police. The Ambit Guards are better suited, equipped, and trained for such occasions and are not hindered by the regulations that plague law enforcement. The taser wands they carry, when used long enough, can dehydrate Earnest."

"What about a trap like the one set for me? I wanted to ask him questions before he ran off."

"I didn't want any traps to potentially or accidentally be used against you. I knew you could handle him with your hand-to-hand skills alone."

"The guards helped out also."

"It was necessary experience for you. I'm sure you can keep him under control until he is no longer a threat."

"Who were those two guards I was with?"

"Often, while working, at least two will accompany you."

"I meant their specific names."

"You can skip their names as they will, in most cases, obey you. The day guards will be dressed more casually to blend in. At night, the Ambit Guards will be in their full uniforms."

"I wouldn't mind having one of those uniforms."

"You'll have time to spend with them later. Have anything to ask about young May?"

"Yes."

Quin took a moment to gather his thoughts. He was excited about Roland being willing to discuss May.

"Did you intentionally take her from me?"

"No."

"You said before that she will never come back to me. I don't agree with that."

"There is a lot to unravel. Do you really want to know why she left you?"

"Yes!"

"Tell me what you believe the possible reason is."

"Maybe because of money?"

"Any other possibilities?"

"Because you're white?"

"I will keep this as superficial as possible. Simply waving cash around will not make anyone worthwhile choose to enter a relationship with someone else. As most worthwhile women mature, they will prefer a partner that not only displays the ability to, but also the knowledge of how, and the willingness to provide."

"But I was working for that. She knew I was."

"May had no faith in your limited successes and lack of resources. The relationship with you was seen as an inevitable failure that she lacked time for. Although she's free to leave me for you, it's unlikely while I am providing for her college and living expenses. She has good reasons to remain with me."

Roland's words reminded Quin about how he couldn't find a meaningful answer to why May would remain with a broke freshman when she had many options.

"You two are going to marry?"

"Your negative feelings stem, in part, from your parents having made you victim to cultural beliefs that rely on peer pressure. In Asian cultures, especially with the Chinese, an unnatural obsession with marriage is commonplace. So unnatural that a woman who is not married by a certain age is labeled a derogatory term that I dare not repeat."

"Yeah, leftover. Is she going to marry you?"

"Living one's life with such a belief creates much room for stressful mistakes. With your powers, you can change your situation for the better. You hurt now because you lack options, but by focusing on success, many more partner opportunities will come to you."

Quin looked at his mask. It made him feel hopeful.

"You may be right, Roland, but I won't give up on her so quickly. Are you two already married?"

"The ability to live alone is given only to a few by God. If you have this gift, it would be wise to use it. Marriage comes with many troubles that I hope you are spared from."

The conversation with Roland only answered a few of Quin's questions. If Quin was to use the mask to better his situation, more information about it was needed. Quin wanted to visit Ashley's house again as soon as possible.

After making his bank deposits, Quin returned after sunset to Mayor Ward's beach house.

Upon arriving, Quin saw more Ambit Guards than before. One of the guards approached Quin with a familiar voice.

"Quin-san! Nice to see you again!"

"It's you! I never caught your name."

"Let's skip that for now. We've just been told to capture Earnest if possible. We will have to set a garlic cheese trap for him. Do you mind removing your mask or returning after an hour so the garlic doesn't affect you?"

"I'd rather keep my mask on. I need to go somewhere anyway. If you catch him, I'd like to question him."

"We will call you if he appears before you return."

Using the powers of his mask, Quin traveled to Ashley's house. It was mostly unchanged from his last visit, except the front door was wide open!

Not knowing what to expect, Quin cautiously entered the house. Inside, the sound of heavy slurping could be heard along with a familiar body odor. The smell led Quin to the same room containing the chest of blood packets.

"Earnest!"

"Draft Dodging Danny?!"

"I was born in the 2000s. I don't think you should be here."

"I just needed blood to use my mask. Who are you?"

"I'll tell you if you tell me where you got the mask you're wearing from."

"Ashley gave it to me."

"Where is she now?"

"At her island. Help me make them pay. Can you use Heaven's Time Zone?"

"I'm Quin, and I have no idea what you're talking about."

"Help me blow them all up! All we need is a Daylight Saving Crystal. I have the bombs ready. Let's go get a crystal from Ward tonight!"

"We just met, but it's clear something is wrong with you, and you're not going near Ward."

"I have to get my revenge against Annalisa. I'll beat you to do it."

"No need to make threats."

"Last time I was thirsty, and you had the guards. This time I drank blood, and you don't have the guards."

"I prefer a fair one on one."

Arms stretched out, Earnest stepped toward Quin with a zombie-like posture while emitting a hiss that matched his rodent-like facial features. Seeing an opening, Quin moved in with a side slam that planted Earnest to the ground.

With rapid wiggling, Earnest scurried away from Quin and out the front door. Matching his speed, Quin followed his target outside to continue the fight.

Earnest's attacks were unconventional, uncoordinated, and unrefined. They were easy for Quin to counter with take downs.

Quin gained the impression that Earnest had zero experience in fighting.

After about a minute of fighting, Earnest started apologizing.

"I'm sorry! I won't do it again!"

"I don't know what's wrong with you, but you need to get out of here and don't come back."

After Earnest escaped into the far distance, Quin remembered that the Ambit guards were planning to capture Earnest. Quin considered pursuing, but he became thirsty during the fight and the smell of the blood packs drew him back inside Ashley's house for a drink.

After quenching his thirst, reflecting on the information received from Earnest greatly intensified Quin's desire to immediately find Ashley.

When Quin resumed searching the house for clues to Ashley's location, the angel's photo caused him to hesitate with fear.

To overcome the fear, Quin forced himself to stare at the picture.

Nothing happened.

Quin turned away and blinked his eyes several times and looked at the photo again.

Still nothing happened.

Regaining his focus, Quin continued searching the house. No clues about Ashley could be found anywhere. The house was a dead end.

Becoming desperate, Quin called Annalisa in a last-ditch effort. Knowing she would not answer, he planned to continuously call until she picked up.

After only a few rings of the first call, Quin was stunned to hear her voice.

"Hiii Quiiin!"

"A-Annalisa?!"

"Nice to hear from you Quin. How are yooou?"

"I—I—I um. Where, um. I just—um."

"Sounds like you don't know what to say. Think about it on your way to the Ward Memorial Park. Don't keep me waiting."

When Quin arrived at the park, he followed the faint smell of Annalisa's perfume to the park's center. He remembered it from riding in her car. When Quin spotted Annalisa, he gasped with excitement.

"Quiiin!"

Annalisa was amazing to Quin, but something was different this time. There was hope.

Remembering Roland's lectures about success, a future partner, and more opportunities made Annalisa seem obtainable.

Annalisa moved closer to hug Quin.

"That mask looks good on you. It fits really well!"

Quin found himself unable to hide his joyous smile at seeing her again as she smiled back.

"You can take that mask off, Quin. I want to see your real face."

After Quin removed his mask, Annalisa hugged him again and kissed him on both cheeks.

"Your ankle is all better! I bet you're glad you visited that psychic now."

"Ha-ha, yeah. It's nice to move freely again—what is this mask she gave me?"

Annalisa's smile and happy demeanor dropped instantly at Quin's question.

"I know you have a lot of questions, Quin. First, tell me what you were doing before you came to me."

"I was at the psychic's house—do you know someone named Earnest? He said he wants revenge against you and something about bombs."

"I do. He wants revenge because he believed we were in a romantic relationship."

"What made him think that?"

"You might find out later. You and your mask could keep me safe from him."

"Of course, I could! He is weak!"

They both laughed.

"Were you hiding from me these past few days? I tried calling and messaging you."

"You needed time alone to get used to the mask."

"Earnest said Ashley gave him the mask he was wearing. I also found blood in Ashley's house and my room. Both of you have masks too!"

Annalisa quietly stared at Quin with a motionless expression.

"What is this mask? Why give this to Earnest and me? What made us so special?"

Annalisa grabbed and interlocked her hand with Quin's and guided him out of the park.

"It would be best if Ashley told you. I can take you to her— tonight."

Chapter 7: Ashley's Island

"How much longer will this drive be?" Quin asked Annalisa. "I don't mean to be impatient, I just really want to know why Ashley gave me something so valuable for free."

Annalisa kept her eyes on the road and responded, "About five minutes."

"I don't want to sound ungrateful because Ashley was right; this mask is solving my problems. But you can imagine I'd want to know why she's helping me of all people, and you won't tell me."

"I don't need to take the risk of you not believing me. Even if I did tell you, you'd still want to hear directly from Ashley, wouldn't you?"

"I suppose you're right."

"Good! I'm glad we finally agree!"

As their ride continued, Annalisa drove Quin to a part of Ward City he'd never seen before. They reached a bridge on a lake's shore that stretched over the water. Fog covered the entire area, making it difficult to see in the distance.

Various signs displayed warnings such as, "Do not enter," "Dead end," "Road Closed," and "Off Limits." Annalisa drove onto the bridge as if the signs didn't exist. Along the bridge, more warning signs for jellyfish, electric eels, and sharks were visible.

Doubting that these animals could live in the same waters, Quin searched the lake on his phone.

The results revealed the lake was located at the old Ward Zoo and Aquarium Island.

Upon reaching the other end of the bridge, the island became apparent. It was encased with thick, tall, and abundant plant life. It could easily be mistaken for an exotic forest.

What came next scared Quin into wearing his mask: a swamp of saltwater crocodiles.

"Annalisa, this place is dangerous!"

Annalisa looked at Quin and then at the reptiles.

"If that crocodile-wrestling Australian could handle them with his bare hands, you surely can with your mask."

Gaining false courage and seeing an opportunity to impress her, Quin told Annalisa to stop the car so he could challenge the reptiles.

"No need," responded Annalisa. "They remain near the coastline and deter people from the island."

"You're right. I already know I can beat them."

"Good! I'm glad we finally agree!"

Quin removed his mask to avoid appearing afraid and quickly changed the topic.

"You promote blood donations and then use the donated blood for yourself. Am I right?"

"Looks like you're becoming quite the detective."

"That way, people come to you without drawing any attention?"

"Close enough."

"What does your mask look like? Can I see it?"

"That's enough investigative journalism; we're here."

With the car moving deeper into the island, building lights became visible through the fog. The buildings were well maintained despite being on a botanically dominated island.

The building where Annalisa parked was clearly a sporting arena. Inside was a small basketball stadium. In the court's center was a wrestling ring.

"This island isn't welcoming enough for a sports team or audience," Quin commented while observing the inside of the arena.

"This island used to be a tourist attraction site. Now only certain people are allowed."

Annalisa stepped inside the wrestling ring and leaned against the ropes, watching Quin as he stood on the outside.

"Remember when I said I'd beat you when your ankle became better, Quin?"

"You were joking."

"You'll lose and admit my sport is real."

"No way," said Quin with a light laugh. "Besides, you're a girl, and I'm a guy."

"Win and I'll show you my mask you asked about earlier."

"Depends. If I win, I beat a woman. If I lose, I lost to a girl. It's a lose-lose for me."

"Maybe, but I think you'll change your mind soon. Ready to meet Ashley?"

"Yes. Ashley is here with us?"

"She's at the food court. Use your mask to follow the scent. While you do that, I'll get everything ready for our fight."

"We're not having a match, Annalisa."

"We'll see."

Quin donned his mask and began to smell a familiar scent. It was the same scent as the blood from his dorm room! The thought of drinking it again made him rush out of the stadium.

The journey to the scent's location exposed more buildings, but Quin ignored them and continued onward.

Arriving at the source of the wonderful fragrance, Quin entered the food court without restraint. The layout of the food court was so typical, it felt familiar to him.

There was no intention of slowing down until he saw her face.

"Hello, Quin dear."

"Ashley!?"

The blood's fragrance caused Quin to forget who he was coming to meet. He wasn't prepared for this moment.

"I'm very glad you could make it tonight, Quin. Please, come sit with me for a drink."

Ashley sat at the head of a banquet table, pointing to an empty seat next to her. In front of her was a tray of fancy, blood-filled glasses. Unable to focus because of the blood's scent, Quin removed his mask to think clearly. He walked to the designated seat while Ashley intently stared at him.

"I'm glad to see the mask has you in a better light, Quin. You look much better compared to our first meeting."

Quin remained silent, contemplating what would motivate Ashley's words.

"When we first met, there was very little I could talk to you about."

Ashley placed a glass of blood in front of Quin before she continued speaking.

"I didn't tell you everything, but what I did tell you was true. Now I can start anew and tell you more. My name really is Ashley Akkadian."

Ashley picked up her glass and held it in the air.

"Welcome to our island! Before we made it one of our homes, it was used as a tourist site."

"Our? We? You and Annalisa?"

"She and my other children."

"I didn't know Annalisa was adopted."

"Generally, an invitation to my family comes after I give someone a mask of my own making."

"Earnest was invited to your family?"

"I said 'generally.'"

Ashley drank from her glass. Quin looked at the glass in front of him and tried to drink from it until Ashley waved her hand at him to stop.

"That's not good to drink without your mask on."

"I saw you drink without a mask."

"My condition is permanent. I don't have a mask to remove like you and my children do."

Quin stared with confusion.

"While wearing the mask, you gain my condition as well as some of my abilities," Ashley continued.

"I need to know why you gave this mask to me."

"To help you with your problems. That should be obvious."

"Of all the people who need help, why me? How does this benefit you?"

Ashley released her fixated stare and began laughing.

"I'm glad you asked, Quin. I would be disappointed if you didn't."

She then drank the rest of the blood from her glass.

"Before I address that," Ashley continued, extending her hand to Quin, "if you feel uncomfortable with the mask, feel free to return it. Or would you rather keep it?"

"I'd—I'd rather keep it." Quin placed a hand on his mask out of fear that Ashley would take it back from him.

"Then I'll offer you a wager. Defeat Annalisa in your upcoming bout, and I will tell you how I benefit from giving you the mask."

"I was being serious!"

"You doubt I'm serious also? Ting, come here, please."

At Ashley's call, a middle-aged man dressed in simple monk robes came to her side. He seemed to have been waiting nearby in one of the food court's kitchens.

"Ting, please introduce yourself and show Mr. High his quarters. Explain the match rules to him as well. Danton will meet you at the hotel and take over from there."

"Yes, ma'am. Mr. High, my name is Ting Asuony of Mexico. I'm Ashley's personal assistant. It is a pleasure to meet you."

"Hey, Ting. Nice to meet you too."

"Please follow me to the parking lot, Mr. High. I'll drive you to your room."

"Mr. High, feel free to change the car's temperature to your liking," said Ting with a heavy Hispanic accent.

"Call me Quin. You seem to be older than me."

"All right," Ting replied, dropping his accent. "What's up, Quin!?"

"That's better. You're one of Ashley's children?"

Ting laughed. "Not at all, I'm not worthy. I'm just in debt to Ashley for getting me out of Riker's Island."

"Speaking of islands, can you tell me about this one?"

"This island was once a zoo, botanical garden, aquarium, and a mall. The hotels allowed overnight stays. Your room will be in the Innocent Inn."

"That's an interesting name, but I don't fit that description."

"Do any of us? It is the most luxurious of the four hotels. The rooms are more spacious and reserved for Ashley's family members. The other three are used as living spaces for the workers, cleaners, and maskless guests."

"I was wondering how the buildings are kept so clean."

"Ashley sent most of them off island to avoid overwhelming you during your first visit. I generally manage and supervise them."

A distraction came from the animals outside the moving truck's window. A gang of kangaroos gripped Quin's attention until they were no longer in view.

"You and Ashley said this 'used' to be a tourist site. Did those crocodiles and oversized kangaroos escape and attack everyone?"

"Before I answer that, I have to explain the rules of your match with Annalisa."

"I don't believe she wants me to fight her. Is this an inside joke I'm unaware of?"

"There are no pinfalls or disqualifications. The only way for you to win is to force Annalisa to say 'It's fake' out loud. If she forces you to say, 'It's real' out loud, you lose."

"The only thing I'll say out loud is that this fight isn't happening."

"There is no time limit, and you may use your mask at any point during the match. Be ready at the arena in an hour from now."

"So why isn't this island a tourist site anymore?"

"I will gladly tell you that story if you defeat Annalisa."

The building lights of the Innocent Inn illuminated the hotel against the night sky. The hotel was impressive enough to make Quin worry whether he could afford to stay at the hotel if he was charged. He was hoping he wouldn't have to spend any of the money he made so far.

At the hotel's entrance stood a man that Quin could not identify. Quin was led by Ting over to the man.

Quin shook hands with an individual of identical height. He sported a head full of wavy hair and refined facial features. He appeared to be in his forties.

"Welcome to the Innocent Inn, Quin! I'm Danton Tolia. This is where Ashley's children stay while on the island."

"Does this mean I'm one of her children now?"

"If you decide to join. I hear you have an upcoming fight with my younger sister. You'll need a room to prepare. Follow me to the elevators and I'll show you to it."

When Danton gestured for Quin to enter the hotel, Ting returned to his vehicle and drove away.

The hotel lobby looked so beautiful that Quin became excited about seeing the room. Danton continued speaking inside the elevator.

"A little bit about myself, I'm one of Ashley's children. I met Ashley back in the 1960s while I was traveling to Canada. I've been with the family ever since. These days, I generally stick close to this island. What about you, Quin? What do you think so far?"

"I met Ashley almost a week ago. Still trying to figure things out."

"Am I right to assume you need more time to process everything?"

"It's all new, stuff I'd only expect to see in movies."

"I understand. We are surrounded by so much fiction these days. It can be hard to notice when it becomes real."

"As far as me fighting Annalisa—I feel like everyone is in on this plot. Are you also?"

"I've known Annalisa for years, and let me tell you, she takes pride in convincing people that her favorite sport can be dangerous."

"With all due respect, that didn't answer the question."

"Look at it as a chance to get familiar with everyone. And I should warn you, you'll need your mask to stand a fair chance against Annalisa. She won't be easy to defeat. Here is your room."

When the two exited the elevator, Danton handed Quin a key card to the door to his room. Once inside, the hotel room made Quin feel as if he were in a large three-bedroom apartment. It was the largest amount of living space he ever had sole access to.

"Wow, this is bigger than my other room!"

"Other room?"

"A guy that I've been working for also gave me a room."

"May I ask who you're working for?"

"Roland Ambit. Have you heard of him?"

"I know that name very well. Real wealthy guy. Pays you a lot, yeah?"

"You know him? What's his story?"

"For now, I have something to show you."

Danton reached into his jacket and pulled out a mask. It was identical to Quin's.

"Our two masks were made at the same time from the same material. Because of this, I'm rooting for you to win the match against Annalisa."

Quin glanced between his own mask and Danton's, noticing differences in their conditions.

"If you're wondering why mine looks discolored and damaged compared to yours, it's because I've bonded with my mask, and the blemishes are proof of that. The stronger your bond with the mask, the stronger you will become while not wearing it. This is why you'll need a mask to win, but Annalisa won't need one to beat you."

As Quin pondered his past battles with the mask, he came to a realization.

"You're Draft Dodging Danny!"

"Ha! You must have already met Earnest."

"I beat him twice while working for Roland. Our masks must have confused him into thinking I was you."

"You beat him twice? Excellent work, Quin! Let's make a deal. Meet us in the arena 30 minutes from now. I'll tell you what I know about Roland—if you defeat Annalisa."

ASHLEY'S CHILDREN

Chapter 8: Quin vs. Annalisa

Quin used the powers of his mask to travel to the arena. He contemplated refusing to show up, but he wanted the information he was seeking from Annalisa, Ashley, Ting and Danton.

Already inside the wrestling ring was Annalisa, striking poses and making faces at Quin. Ting stood inside also, holding a microphone. Ashley and Danton sat in the bleachers. They were both smiling.

Doubting he would need it, Quin tucked his mask into his hoodie pocket. He planned to end the fight quickly and then blame his victory on Annalisa's arrogance.

Quin entered the ring and took a deep breath.

"Quin," Ting said, "This fight may be monitored or recorded for quality and training purposes."

"There are only two audience members, and I don't see any cameras anywhere," Quin said doubtfully.

"If you believe that, you can give up now," interjected Annalisa. She took the microphone from Ting and placed it in front of Quin. "Say it. Say, 'It's real' now to save yourself some pain!"

"Remember, if you win, I'll tell you what I know about Roland!" Danton shouted from the bleachers.

Quin took the microphone from Annalisa and threw it down. "I don't want to hurt you, so I'll beat you without my mask."

Annalisa responded with a swift slap across Quin's face, nearly knocking him off his feet. When Quin looked up, another slap followed that caused him to fall to the mat.

Ting placed himself between Annalisa and Quin and asked Quin if he wanted to continue.

Choking prevented Quin from making a fast recovery. After coughing for a few seconds, the source of the choke was revealed to be his own wisdom tooth.

"Uh-oh," Annalisa said, "looks like you got a boo-boo. Get up so I can give you more!"

Remembering the stakes of victory, Quin placed his mask on.

For the next few minutes, it gradually became difficult for Quin to maintain a suitable defense against Annalisa's offense despite having his mask on. The fight became increasingly one sided against him. He didn't feel as powerful as before and he wasn't healing much.

Annalisa seemed more interested in putting on a show rather than winning.

After several theatrical takedowns, Quin was trapped with both arms pulled behind him and a knee being driven into his back.

"Say it, Quin!"

"This fight isn't over yet!"

"That tooth I knocked out will grow back, but your arms won't. Say it!"

"Okay! It's real!" Quin shouted after feeling multiple pops in his arms and back.

"Danny doesn't have his mask on. Say it louder!"

"It's real! It's real!"

Chapter 9: The First Son

Quin and Danton remained silent during their drive back to the Innocent Inn. They didn't speak until they were alone in Quin's room.

"If my healing hadn't slowed down, I would've won!"

"Your abilities aren't as effective when you're dehydrated. You may have been too focused on getting answers to notice you were thirsty. When was the last time you drank blood or ate food?"

Quin felt regret while remembering he never drank with Ashley while at the food court.

"I would have won if I drank earlier!"

"I doubt it. It takes time for your body to adjust to the mask and become stronger."

"If you doubted, why did you make a deal with me?"

"I had to give you a chance. Besides, it's more important that you know the importance of staying hydrated. In addition, know that Annalisa did sneak her mask on during the latter half of the fight."

"I didn't see a mask on her face."

"Her mask is more discreet than ours. It's a pair of fangs that are easy to hide. Don't feel bad for losing to her."

"If you were in my position, you'd understand better; the answers I need have slipped away from me."

"Don't fret. There's a chance to redeem yourself tonight. We are setting a trap for Earnest. It would be an opportunity to add another win onto your record and to learn more about the family."

"What kind of trap?"

"You, Ting, Ashley, and I will sit as bait inside the warehouse. When Earnest comes, you defeat him and lock him inside a cage."

"Sounds easy. Can't say 'no' to that, I guess."

"Great! I'll come get you in an hour and show you where we'll be. Be sure to drink before I return."

"Looking forward to it. I could use another win. I hope it's also monitored and recorded for quality and training purposes."

Danton laughed and asked if Quin had any more questions.

"I just noticed that I was never able to smell anyone's blood in the arena. Why is that?"

"You won't be able to smell the blood of Ashley or another mask user. Ting uses a special spray and vaccine that prevents his blood from giving off a scent," Danton explained. "It prevents Ashley and the rest of us from being tempted to drink his blood. I can tell you more when we gather together for Earnest's trap. Annalisa won't be there, but there will be another person present that you'll be interested in meeting. You'll get to meet Ashley's first son."

At the warehouse, Quin sat at a round table with Ashley, Ting, and Danton. Danton told a story while they waited for Earnest.

"I came of age during the Vietnam draft. Back then I was part of the Mormon church. Not many people know this, but the Church of Latter Day Saints could provide draft exemptions for its missionaries. I was relying on this, but by the time I received my draft notice, the government placed limits on the number of exemptions the Mormons could give. My Greek roots made me indifferent about joining the U.S. military. After seeking counsel, I decided to leave for Canada. While preparing to leave, I found out that my girlfriend was pregnant. I wanted to bring her with me, but I was low on cash, and her family didn't want her running off with me. That's when Ashley came and gave me my mask."

"But you two look way too young for those days," said Quin.

"The masks slow our aging. To give you an idea, Ashley met the first son during the first World War."

Quin couldn't create a response because Ashley appeared younger than Danton.

"Speaking of my eldest, he is the last one we are waiting for. While we wait, care to learn about the trap's victim, Quin, dear?"

"Yes," Quin quickly replied.

"When we first saw Earnest, he was around 25 years old and still living off his mother. He didn't finish high school and worked a job that didn't even pay him minimum wage. He was a single child, and his single mother wanted him out of her apartment after deeming him a complete failure. When she unexpectedly became ill and disabled, she kept Earnest around since her only other family was her sister. She and her sister hated each other with a screaming passion."

Quin's concentration was interrupted by a rumbling noise coming from the ceiling. Ashley motioned for him to ignore it and continued.

"Seeing an opportunity, I instructed Annalisa to enter a false courtship with Earnest to persuade him into becoming a test subject for my 'science' experiments. My plan worked. He fell wholeheartedly in love with my daughter. His mother, unaware of the truth, was suspicious. However, seeing her son with someone as great as my daughter gave her hope that her child wasn't a complete loss, and that she might even get new family members."

The noise from the ceiling continued. Quin could sense it was coming from the vents above them.

"After we finished the experiments, my daughter ended the courtship. Earnest was less than happy. Commitment standards are so low this decade that Earnest felt Annalisa was committed to him because she often prepared his favorite dish of scrambled eggs on tomato and rice. Now Earnest is seeking vengeance against us."

Quin's mouth dropped open, his eyes widening in shock and awe. It took several seconds before he could regain his composure.

"My first two times meeting him make more sense now," Quin said with a tone of pity. "I think he plans on using bombs. Why all of you and not just Annalisa?"

"He falsely believed he was part of my family and felt betrayed by us all when no one stood up for him. The masks my children use are made of a very special material. Earnest's mask was part of the experiments he subjected himself to in the name of true love."

"That's what watching too many fairy tale movies will do to you," injected Danton with a laugh.

"Something is really not right with that guy," Quin said.

"He was fine when he was harassing my sister after she dumped him," Danton shot back.

"The mask Earnest wears isn't the same as my children's," Ashley said. "His mask was specifically designed to change him into—my first born is here. Ting, could you open the door for him, please?"

Ting stood up from the table where they were sitting at and walked to a nearby door.

"Quin," said Danton, "this is my older brother and the first son!"

When the door opened, the person standing on the other side sent shock throughout Quin's entire body.

It was Roland Ambit.

"Mr. High, we have much to discuss."

Quin wanted to re-evaluate the last week of his life as Roland calmly joined everyone at the table.

Quin shifted his eyes to everyone in the room numerous times while they quietly watched him in silence as if they were expecting a reaction. The noise from the ceiling vents continued to grow louder.

After a full minute passed, Roland broke the silence. "Quin, there will be time to piece everything together. For now, I need you to act as an exterminator for our rat infestation."

"Quin, dear, while you didn't defeat my daughter, I know you'd still like to know my motives for giving you the mask. Defeat the rodent, and I will gladly tell you."

After another moment passed, a familiar character grabbed Quin's attention.

"Quin-san!"

It was the Ambit Guard that Quin met the night of Jason Ward's wedding. His uniform was different now. It now bore the number 10 on the shoulders.

Drawing everyone's attention to the ceiling, Ashley snapped her fingers. The vents then split open, causing a body, mail packages, a detonation trigger, and a baseball bat to fall to the ground.

It was Earnest.

Ashley opened her hand towards the direction of the detonation trigger. The trigger flew off the ground into her hand. After briefly observing it, she extended her hand again and the packages also flew towards her.

Earnest stood up and looked at everyone in horror.

"Oops. Can I? Can I have my bombs back, please?"

"Quin, subdue him. The 10th, Ting, get the transport cage ready," ordered Roland. "Our unwanted guest could benefit from another session in the Processing Plant."

Mask on, Quin turned and faced his target. Excited about getting questions answered and redeeming his loss to Annalisa, Quin fought Earnest.

Earnest tried fighting back to no avail. Even being armed with a baseball bat didn't help. At Danton's instruction, Quin continued the attack until Earnest stopped resisting and started apologizing.

"I knew you could best him on your own," cheered Ashley. "Ting, The 10th, unmask and cage Earnest."

Ashley and her two sons guided Quin back to the table's seat. They all watched as the Ambit Guard struck Earnest with a taser baton until his rat-like mask fell off his face.

Next, the guard and Ting tossed Earnest's body into a large metal crate labeled "*Ward Zoo.*"

Ashley extended her hand, causing Earnest's mask to fly toward her.

When the cage's door was locked, Danton and Ashley walked towards it and stared at Earnest.

"Mom, can we taunt and lecture him?"

"Of course, son," replied Ashley with a smile.

"Bum! The mask you thought you stole from me was a fake!" Danton shouted to Earnest. "That's how we knew about your plans! You thought stealing my mask would make it easier for you to steal Jason's Daylight Saving Crystal at his wedding. You plan failed at every angle."

"I know what I did wrong," Earnest said from inside the cramped cage. "I won't do it again."

"That's what you said after the first time you were processed," Ashley replied. "Your predictable failure is a consequence of your overwhelming incompetence. If that's too complex for you to understand—you never had a chance."

Quin wanted to feel sorry for Earnest, but remembering the bombs Earnest brought made Quin realize that Earnest was best locked in a cage.

"Ting, the 10th, take him to the Processing Plant! Be sure to load it with bread first so our guest can spend some extra time in there," Ashley commanded.

After the Ambit Guard and Ting pushed the crate out of view, Quin resumed silently pondering and processing all the information he had just received. He was so lost in thought that it took him several seconds to realize Ashley was speaking to him.

"Quin, dear, you have a lot to think about. But first—Danton, give it to him now, please."

Danton handed Quin a $1000 check. "There's the other half of your pay. Now you know what I know about Roland."

Quin smiled joyfully.

"It's wonderful to see you happy, Quin," said Ashley. "Concerning the mask, and how I benefit, I will tell you tomorrow night. It's early morning now. It'd be best if you got some rest in your new room and gather your thoughts because after the next sunset, I will invite you to our family."

Quin awoke the next afternoon with a headache from the revelation of Ashley and Roland being connected. Only by coming to a conclusion was Quin motivated to get out of bed. His conclusion was that his break-up with May was planned.

After scanning through multiple concerned text messages from class and teammates, Quin tried calling Roland to confirm his conclusion. However, the poor reception he was receiving in the area made it impossible.

A few moments later Quin heard his room's phone ringing. It was Roland.

"Young Quin, meet me downstairs in our hotel's lobby area where we'll discuss any concerns you have."

When Quin entered the lobby, a relaxed Roland sat at a lounge table. He seemed prepared to meet.

"Before we begin, Quin, I have some good news. Mayor Ward's brother was able to withdraw you from all your classes, and your student loans have been taken care of. All of your belongings will be taken to your motel in the city."

Quin's face showed strong disapproval towards Roland's words.

"You just took away my education! What will I do now if I get injured? A degree was my backup plan!"

"Were you not injured before receiving the mask that healed you? Now you know why Jesus always had such large crowds."

Quin calmed down at the thought of being able to heal any future injuries with his mask.

"My life has gotten better with this mask, but it wasn't right to plot to take May from me. Seeing you, May, and Annalisa at the Ambit Inn was my first clue. I should have seen the link between you and Ashley through Annalisa and Earnest. May didn't want to leave me! You all took her from me!"

"Ashley and Annalisa did not cause your separation, but rather they accelerated it. May's feelings were not injected, but rather exposed. Ashley used that opportunity to provide compelling incentive for you to wear the mask."

"You sound like you were not involved, but you were the main problem."

"Your situation was so vulnerable it was easy for Ashley—so easy that I was unaware of her plans until last night. I initially thought you stole your mask or received it from somewhere other than Ashley. When Annalisa introduced May to me, it was for other reasons."

"I don't want to be upset, I don't like being upset, but I am upset. Even if you weren't aware, I'm upset that May isn't with me. You could now change the situation."

"Young May wasn't forced to leave you. She was merely unaware of her options before meeting me—while you remained with her because you lacked options. For women, one wrong mate selection can become a life-ruining decision, and May felt this way about you. Rather than waste it, Ashley changed your preexisting and inevitable depression into a positive outcome for everyone."

"There's no way anyone could have known that. That's an assumption. I still had time to fix things!"

"Partnerships often end in failure when at least one partner didn't get who or what they wanted; instead, they settled for what was accessible to them. It was a confirmed case when May revealed to Annalisa that she imagined the vehicle you planned to purchase her would be used and missing hubcaps."

Quin sighed in frustration with a range of emotions plaguing his thoughts.

"I don't think me being depressed was necessary."

"That suffering was needed to attract you to the mask. Ever since you accepted it, you are no longer powerless, no longer broke, no longer optionless, and if you join our family, no longer alone."

Quin leaned back and took a deep breath, reflecting on the money and friends to be made through the mask.

His thoughts pondered on his parents' reaction to him having a big bank account and giving them grandchildren. A welcome back would be guaranteed.

"I am definitely joining your family," he said.

"That's the proper attitude to have!"

"Since you are the first son, I won't get any inheritance. I can start from the ground up and start my own extension?"

"This family is much more generous and cohesive than what your used to. You will receive so much that you may forget you are not the eldest son."

"That sounds relieving. New and relieving."

"The 10th will retrieve you from your quarters tonight and bring you to the conference room where you will be offered an invitation to our family."

"The 10th?"

"The 10th Ambit Knight. I will have him explain and introduce himself to you. Until then, feel free to explore the island. The fog and dense trees will protect you from the sunlight during the day."

ASHLEY'S CHILDREN

Chapter 10: The Angel That Manifests

When night came, the Ambit Guard who caged Earnest the previous night knocked on Quin's door. His uniform was still different from the first night they met.

"Quin-san! Are you ready for Ashley's invitation?" he asked.

"Hey, Ambit Guard. I never caught your name."

"Call me 'The 10th.' My real name is top secret."

"Your uniform looks different from the other night. I think it's cool."

"Thanks! I work hard to look good and get noticed. Before, I was working undercover as a standard guard in a silver lettered uniform. My actual title is 'The 10th Ambit Knight.' The knights have the gold lettered uniforms like my current one."

"I want a uniform like that."

"Danton can get one for you, but first we should head to the car. Be sure to bring your mask with you."

After they both entered the vehicle, the 10th continued speaking.

"The Ambit Knights are the ranking officers for Ambit Services— just under Ashley's children. There are ten of us total, ranked by seniority with the 1st Knight being the most senior and the 10th being the newest. We were all either prior commissioned military officers, special forces, or federal agents. If you decide to join the family, I'll be assigned to you."

"That's really cool! Which one were you?"

"Naval officer. I can tell you more after the invitation. Until then, bear with me as I drive through this night fog. I'm taking you to the Botanical Garden's conference room."

"Do any of the Ambit Knights or Guards get masks?"

"No, only Ashley's children. Once you finish with the invitation, you and I will have to fetch Earnest from the Processing Plant. That will be our first assignment together and a chance to impress Ashley."

"A terrorist in a processing plant?"

"He's not being ground up like chicken or anything. When we get him out of it, I'll explain."

"Since you're coming along, the invitation is public?"

"No. Only Ashley and her children will be there. Apparently, there is a certain person you'll meet that only Ashley and her children are allowed to see. I won't be allowed inside."

At the botanical garden, Quin followed the 10th to the conference room. Remaining focused was difficult with colorful and exotically shaped plants at every turn. Distracted by a display of plants shaped like jellyfish and an overgrown cactus, Quin almost lost his guide.

The 10th departed after showing Quin the conference room's doors. Quin entered to see Ashley at the head of a conference table. Sitting with her at the table was Roland, Danton and Annalisa.

"I saved you a seat next to me, Quin dear," said Ashley. Quin sat in the assigned seat with a nervous twist from seeing Annalisa for the first time since their fight.

"My first son tells me you are eager to join our family. We're so happy to hear it."

Roland silently smiled at Quin.

"Before I invite you, this is an ideal time to air any negative feelings you may have about my involvement in your relationship with May."

"I'd rather keep that private," Quin said, glancing at Ashley's children.

"Understood. Children, give us some time alone, please."

After Roland, Danton, and Annalisa left the room, Quin focused his attention on Ashley.

"At first, I wasn't happy about it," he said, "but it turned out better for me. What I lost can be replaced."

"Great," said Ashley with a smile. "You're on the right path. Even so, I know you're still attached to May."

"You're right. To be honest, after I join your family, I'm going back for her. Now that I have the mask, I can get her back."

"Although you deserve better, one week isn't enough time to change your flawed and desperate way of thinking. It will only change once you've gotten used to being desirable. Until then, I will arrange for you to meet with May again."

"No! Don't do that! I'll do it alone!"

"You'll need some sort of assistance. Currently, May is committed to Roland and has no incentive to communicate with you. It may be a long time before she leaves Roland."

"Just—just please forget I said anything about May. Forget I mentioned her."

"Ready to learn what I have to gain?"

"Yes, please."

"You have never heard of this before. I chose you over others because you were chosen to live a different life than most people. You and my children were destined to discover the truth of life—not to live in lies like the world does. This makes you extremely valuable."

Ashley paused and stared at Quin as Quin stared back, doubting her words.

"The mask I gave you comes with a price. Continue using it, and you will NOT be able to enter Heaven. However, if you and my children continue using the masks, I can bargain our way out of eternal trouble on Judgment Day."

"That is odd and intense," replied Quin with confusion. "Almost unbelievable."

"To put it differently, by joining my family, I can keep you and my other children safe from punishment. You can continue using the mask without worry."

Quin thought about Ashley's words until a disturbing thought came to his mind.

"That means Annalisa's plan all along was to get me to join your family."

"Whether it be for new family members, new blood donors, or new test subjects, Annalisa is a talented recruiter that only a few can resist."

Quin took a moment of silence upon hearing Ashley imply that Annalisa was staging him for this moment. He felt like a fool and wanted to quickly change the subject.

"The Heaven part, that's more of your religion and department. I believe a bit differently. If you believe that, why not tell me before?"

"When we first met, you didn't believe anything I said to you. The events from then and now were necessary to open your mind. You likely would not have tried the mask at all had I mentioned that to you."

Quin remained silent, lacking a proper response. A part of him knew Ashley was right.

"I tell you these things now because you need to understand the full cost of that mask, Quin."

Quin stared at his mask for a few moments, thinking about Ashley's words. When he looked towards her again, she continued speaking.

"I have informed you that continuing to use the mask will make it impossible for you to go to Heaven," she warned, extending her hand towards Quin in a receiving posture. "If the cost is too great, you can give the mask back and go back to your old life. Or would you like to keep it and join my family?"

Quin paused for a moment and responded, "I'm not going back to my old life. I want to join."

Ashley smiled and stood up. At the wave of her hand, Quin felt himself being lifted out of his seat into a standing position. Quin's mask fell onto the table. Ashley then wrapped her arms around him for a tight hug.

Quin tried to pull away, but her grip was too strong.

"I'm so happy you made the right choice, my dear Quin!"

Quin continued trying to break free, but her hug only became tighter. He wanted to wear his mask to gain enough strength to escape Ashley's grip, but his arms were trapped in the hug.

When Ashley finally released him, Quin heard clapping coming from the direction behind them.

"Quin! Quin! Quin!"

Confused by the new and unfamiliar voice, Quin turned around to see a very tall, hooded figure dressed in semi-monk robes with a hoodie clapping its hands.

"Magnificent Choice, Quin."

Quin tried to meet the figure's eyes but couldn't, due to the shadow over its face. It seemed to be about eight feet tall with intensely dark skin.

"You Can Call Me 'Tansafo,'" said the figure, who was clearly a male. He spoke with a comedic, yet realistic tone.

Quin stared harder at the face, shifting his head's positions hoping to get a glimpse of the man's face. The room's lighting was fine, but

Quin couldn't see anything but a shadow. Hesitant because of its towering height, Quin slowly inched closer. When close enough, Quin gasped in horror. There was no face under the hood. Quin was staring into a dark void.

"Wear Your Mask For A Proper Introduction."

Feeling fearful, Quin did as he was told. After masking, Quin felt a familiar sensation.

Quin fell to his knees and his eyes fixated on the figure—unable to look away or move. Time seemed to stand still as his vision steadily blurred to black. As the blur intensified, words formed in the middle of the darkness:

"THE ANGEL THAT MANIFESTS"

When the letters and darkness disappeared, Quin realized that he was kneeling and breathing heavily.

Able to move again, Quin stood and turned to Ashley. She stared back at him, seemingly unaware of Tansafo. Tansafo's next words would forcefully regain Quin's attention:

"With My Right Hand,

I Remove The Thorn And Give It To The Fatherless.

With My Left Hand,

I Inspire Awe For A Decade Times Decades.

The Inheritance Of A Dead Language.

Sell All You Have For The Price Of Life."

Through much confusion, Quin asked, "What?"

"Don't Worry About It Kid, That Was Just My Fourth Chant."

When Tansafo finished speaking, a bright light flashed that knocked Quin unconscious.

When Quin's eyes opened, he sat alone at the conference room table.

Quin remembered what happened before he blacked out, but there was no trace of Ashley or the angel. He estimated he was unconscious for 10 minutes.

While Quin wondered if Tansafo was real or a dream, Ashley entered the conference room. She carried a flask of deliciously smelling blood with her.

She placed the flask next to Quin; he drank until there was no more.

Ashley watched Quin without saying a word. She seemed to be waiting for him to say something. Quin wanted to ask her what knocked him unconscious, but he remembered that she didn't seem aware of Tansafo. He chose not to mention it.

"Thank you. I think I blacked out from being thirsty."

"You were talking to something before you collapsed. The Ambit Guards reported you were talking to yourself while you were protecting Ward's wedding. Want to share that experience with me?"

"I don't remember doing that, but I'll be more careful."

To avoid shame, Quin changed the topic. "What do you call that special blood I was given at my dorm? How can I get more?"

"Although I've been spoiling you with it to expedite your joining of my family, we usually celebrate by drinking it when a new member is added to our family. However, it will have to wait since we have a guest in the Processing Plant. The 10th is waiting outside to take you there to fetch Earnest and lock him in the dungeons below the zoo. After that, we can drink the tea blood together."

"The 10th said that the Knights and Guards take orders from Ashley's children."

"Yes. This is your chance to know him better. He will be assigned to you for at least six months. Just as the senior enlisted teach the junior officers, he will help you assimilate."

Quin contemplated telling Ashley about the angel. He wanted to forget it as a dream, but unlike a dream, he remembered every detail and the words of nonsense that Tansafo spoke.

Chapter 11: Bankruptcy

"Quin-san! I'm officially assigned to you! I'm your Ambit Knight! Ashley's tasked me with taking you to the Processing Plant. It's located here, in the botanical garden."

"It's an actual plant?"

"Yes. We have to get Earnest from there and take him to the zoo's dungeon. Please follow me."

After navigating through the botanical garden's interior, Quin and the 10th entered a large dome tent. Inside were massive carnivorous plants; some of which were taller than Quin. Each held Quin's attention for several moments, especially the plants bearing fruit.

The 10th patiently waited while Quin marveled at the garden.

"Can plants that eat bugs also make fruit?"

"Ashley takes joy in creating meat-eating plants that can produce fruit," the 10th responded. "It's her version of gardening. She is an impressive woman."

Quin continued observing the garden until one plant in the center stole his attention. It stood about 20 feet tall. The flower portion was closed with long finger-like petals. Its stem and roots mimicked a pitcher plant that was large enough to swallow a cow.

Quin followed the path to the plant and stared at it. The plant, seemingly aware of Quin, slowly turned its head toward him. Quin felt like the plant was staring back.

"This must be the Processing Plant," Quin stated.

"Ashley created it and uses it as a form of punishment. She got the idea from a guy who was stuck inside some type of sea creature for three days. Earnest is inside it now."

"The Prison Plant would be a better name."

"The plant tries to digest whatever is inside it. That's why it's called *processing.* Whatever it cannot digest will be regurgitated after about 20-24 hours. It cannot digest an adult human."

Growling noises from the plant prevented Quin from responding. The 10th stepped over to a nearby shelf with gardening tools. He grabbed a water hose and a box of baking soda and carried them over to the plant.

"That growling sound means we've got about five minutes before Earnest is released," continued the 10th. "I've got this water hose ready to wash him down when he's out. Any questions for me?"

"I have many. Tell me your name."

"While I follow your orders, the orders of Ashley and Roland still take priority. We are to keep our real names a secret. Want to see my face?"

"Yes."

The 10th placed the water hose on the ground and removed his ski mask. Once removed, it revealed an African American man with black kiss tattoos on his face.

Quin didn't want to appear rude by asking about the tattoos, but he couldn't resist.

"Do all the guards have tattoos under their masks?"

"The Ambit Knights and select guards. Ashley does this to keep us obedient."

"She pays for tattoos in exchange for loyalty?"

"Not at all," said the 10th with a laugh. "This isn't a tattoo, it's more like a curse we must accept since we are trusted with more of the family's secrets. It inspires us to remain loyal to Ashley's family. I think it's worth it considering this beautiful uniform we get. The ski masks hide the marks. Going to the bank is a nightmare!"

"What do your parents and family say about it?"

"Being single with no dependents is a requirement for the Ambit Knights and most guards. We're paid enough to care for our parents remotely with caretakers. Ashley is the only parent I need direct contact with."

"That's wild! I could never do that to my parents!"

"Ahh, sorry, that's the Kiss of Servitude talking—or is it? Anyways, we focus our time on your family and looking good in this uniform."

Quin wanted to respond, but movement from the Processing Plant stopped him.

"Quin-san, I'm going to wash Earnest with this hose to knock off the odor."

The flower end of the Processing Plant began to bloom. When it fully opened, Earnest slid from the bloom's center and fell to the ground. He smelled like spoiled milk and dog droppings.

While the 10th sprayed him with the water hose, Earnest remained on the ground. Quin expected Earnest to try escaping, but Earnest did not resist at all. After a few minutes of spraying, the 10th poured the box of baking soda on Earnest and sprayed him again with the water hose.

"Washing him with water once won't be enough to get rid of that horrible smell. It usually takes about two or three days of showering with baking soda to get rid of it."

After taking turns spraying Earnest with water for another few minutes, the 10th and Quin put Earnest back inside the same animal cage from the previous night and transported him to the zoo's underground dungeon where they locked him inside a cell. Although the cell was intended to hold animals, it was very similar to a jail cell.

"Ashley will be happy with us, Quin-san! She wants you to wait here so you can see the experiment she'll conduct on Earnest. I got a radio message from Roland saying to meet him at the aquarium."

"Before you go, don't you get hot wearing that jacket in all black? The weather is getting warmer."

"Sometimes you gotta be hot to look hot."

Chapter 12: Hearing Voices

When the 10th arrived at the aquarium, he could not find Roland. At the aquarium's entrance doors, he saw a white mask and a duffle bag with three blood flasks next to it. He attempted to report it to Roland until he heard a comedic voice from above.

"Don't Return That Mask To Ashley!"

"Who's there?! Who said that?!"

"It's Me, Your Conscience."

"I've never heard you before."

"That's Because Your Kiss Of Servitude Has Just Been Dulled. We Can Speak Together Now."

"Conscience huh? Then what's my greatest worry?"

"That Ashley Will Never Love You."

"But, if I use this mask I just found to become stronger, then Ashley will love me."

"Exactly! I'll Make A Distraction So You Can Escape The Island."

"Yes! Then I can train to outshine Ashley's children!"

"That's Using The Ol' Noodle!"

"I'm a genius!"

"I Wouldn't Go That Far."

Inside the zoo dungeon, Earnest remained silent.

Feeling thirsty, Quin considered drinking some of Earnest's blood, but he still smelled disgusting.

Quin removed his mask to escape the temptation. Doing so shifted his thirst to hunger. He planned to leave and search for something to eat until he saw Ashley and Annalisa coming down the stairwell.

"Absolutely brilliant work, child! You did exactly what your big sister and I needed," Ashley said while moving toward Earnest's cell.

"Here, brother," said Annalisa, handing Quin a packet of blood, "You'll want to stick around for this."

"Daughter, before we begin, wash your future slave again; he still reeks from being processed."

Annalisa retrieved a water hose from a nearby cleaning closet and blasted Earnest with it. Quin donned his mask and drank from his blood packet while watching.

When Annalisa finished, Ashley levitated Earnest towards the cell's bars and stabbed an injection needle into his arm.

"I forgot to clean this needle but who cares when it's being used on you? The good news is that this experiment won't be as painful as the others—at least not in the beginning."

Earnest didn't respond as the last drop of fluid entered his body.

"What I put into your body is highly addictive and famous for ruining lives, families, and communities. I'd best explain your mistakes now before it lowers your intelligence even further."

Earnest's expression became relaxed and sleepy.

"When my daughter first approached you, you were never suspicious. My daughter is amazing—you are not. Your desperation and lack of self-awareness blinded you from pondering why you were chosen over better choices."

Earnest moved to the back of the cell and sat down. He seemed tired.

"Your second mistake was allowing my daughter to learn your personal preferences. Strangers showing an interest in your interest without revealing their motives, are likely plotting something."

Earnest silently stared at the ceiling. He clearly wasn't interested in what Ashley had to say.

"Your third mistake was believing that my daughter shared the same feelings you had for her. She did little in exchange for you consenting to my experiments, but you still agreed to them."

Listening to Ashley, Quin reflected on his own time spent with Annalisa.

"Your fourth mistake was allowing the experiments to continue. They negatively impacted your appearance over time."

"This guy isn't interested. I think she's really talking to me!"

"Yes, Quin, this is for you. It's less painful to study the mistakes of others rather than your own."

Quin covered his mouth to prevent more outbursts.

"I don't completely blame you, Earnest," continued Ashley. You didn't know that to have better in life, you must become better yourself. You fell victim to the belief that you shouldn't compare yourself to others. The problem is that others are constantly comparing others to you."

"Can I go? I promise this time I won't do it again."

"I'm not as gullible as you are, Earnest. We'll be back later to give you another injection."

Earnest curled into a ball on the floor.

Annalisa laughed. When Quin looked at her trying to figure out what was funny, she replied, "He will want more of those injections so badly that he will be willing to work hard all day and night for them."

A part of Quin still felt bad for Earnest, who lay snoring in his cell.

Ashley put her arm around Quin's shoulders. "Quin, while it is obvious that Earnest has severe mental issues, that isn't a defense from my perspective. He knew what he did was wrong. When we confronted him, his first words were 'oops.' He even promised that he would not do anything against us again. He did the same thing when he spent a year in jail for assaulting someone with a baseball bat."

"You're right," said Quin in agreement. "He's dangerous."

"Good! I'm glad we finally agree," Annalisa inserted.

Ashley smiled and levitated Quin up the exit stairs behind her. Annalisa followed them as Quin flailed his arms and legs trying to escape Ashley's levitation grip.

A few moments after Earnest was no longer in view, Quin stopped struggling against Ashley's levitation grip when he heard a familiar comedic voice speaking in the zoo dungeon:

"Get Up And Eat."

When Ashley, Annalisa, and Quin reached the zoo's surface entrance, Ashley released Quin from her levitation grip and handed Annalisa a piece of paper.

"I understand, Mother," said Annalisa after reading the note. Annalisa then gave Quin a good-bye hug and left.

"Your big sister will be using her influence to get more blood donors from Ward University. We'll have our celebration drink without her."

Hearing the word "celebrate" excited Quin about the tea blood.

"Let's get to the warehouse where you can wait with Roland and Danny while Ting finishes preparing the beverages."

Quin remained forcefully silent. His thoughts were split between how to stop speaking his inner thoughts aloud, how Ashley was able to levitate him and the voice he heard coming out of the zoo dungeon. He believed Ashley would stop him if he tried going back downstairs and he didn't know how to escape her levitation grip. His pondering didn't stop until Ashley spoke again.

"Let's race to the warehouse, Quin. I want to see how swiftly you can move."

"Sorry, I didn't catch that."

"Let's see if you can reach the warehouse before me."

Quin held his hand over his mouth to ensure he would not speak his next idea out loud.

If I can get her away from here, I can run back downstairs while she's distracted.

Quin removed his hand from his mouth and said, "I'll win."

"Let's make it interesting. Get there first and I'll give you the recipe for the tea blood."

"Then I'll be able to fish for life!"

"If I win, you'll have to call me 'Mommy' for a month."

"Deal! I'm ready!"

"We'll take the road under the streetlights. Go!"

Quin sprinted full speed ahead.

Realizing he was in the lead, Quin looked back to see where Ashley was. She was still at the starting spot. She hadn't moved at all.

Quin stopped to figure out why she wasn't moving. Ashley still didn't move. She just motioned for him to continue moving forward.

Seeing an easy win, Quin resumed running.

Quin struggled to stay focused amidst groups of peacocks, pangolins, and porcupines along the way.

When Quin reached the warehouse, Ashley could not be seen anywhere. Quin waited for her in the parking lot next to the golf carts.

I must be faster than her already.

Looking at his phone, Quin estimated it took him about a minute to travel the mile-long distance.

The entire island now felt smaller to him.

When Quin looked back up, he saw Ashley calmly walking toward him.

"Since you're already this fast, I won't take it easy on you next time," Ashley said grinning at Quin.

Quin removed his mask, smiling back so she could see his face.

The two laughed together.

Before Ashley and Quin reached the building's entrance door, Roland and Danton exiting out of it.

"Sons, where are you going? Is this not the time for Quin's first family drink?"

"The senior Knights have requested an emergency meeting with Danny and me."

"What has happened that cannot wait?"

"They claim to have encountered our cousins and then stopped communicating."

"Wait," interrupted Quin. "If the story of your nieces and nephews was true, will they hate me also?"

Ashley, Roland and Danton looked at Quin for a long moment then resumed talking.

"I know my children are capable but always be careful. Call often and don't keep me worried."

"Of course, Mother," said Danton. "And before you ask, we already ate a high iron diet, and the 10th packed enough for us to drink."

"I suppose we can delay my youngest child's commemoration for another day."

"Look on the bright side," continued Danton. "This will give you time to get more of our siblings together. Then after that I can show Quin how to put his mask to good use!"

"Good thinking. I'd rather do it when I know you're safe and well," Ashley stated with a relieved tone.

"Young Quin, while Danton and I are away, you will be the man of the island," said Roland. "You are to keep it and our mother safe."

"Roland! Don't tell him that so soon! He's just a boy and has many questions," Ashley exclaimed.

"He's not a journalist," Danton protested. "Give him room to spread his wings. Otherwise, he'll never get stronger."

"This would be excellent experience and an opportunity for him to display his talents," stated Roland in agreement with Danton.

"Just hurry back. I don't want to lose any of my children."

Ashley hugged Roland, Danton and Quin.

"Quin," Ashley continued, "I'll try not to worry. I'll be working in my quarters. I'll give you the tea blood recipe soon."

Ashley got inside one of the nearby golf carts and drove away. When she was gone, Quin spoke to Roland and Danton.

"I don't mind calling everyone '*brother*' and '*sister*,' but I don't feel right calling her '*mom*.' I still have a mother."

"We don't expect you to," said Danton. "We know you still have parents, but Ashley does love you like her own and we do see you as our brother."

"She respects your respect for your birthparents. She'd rather you refer to her as '*mom*' only if you feel comfortable," Roland added.

"There is something I need to ask about. While I was alone with Ashley at the botanical garden, I saw a really tall guy about eight feet with—"

The trio's attention was taken by an incoming car. The driver was the 10th. He parked and spoke to Roland and Danton.

"To Ward City?"

"Yes, 10th. Drive us to the helicopter there and we will fly to the office," replied Roland. "Quin, we will have to discuss who you saw another time. I have written you a letter of encouragement. It is waiting in your Innocent Inn room. I hope it helps."

Danton smiled at Quin and said, "I look forward to showing you how cool your mask can be. We will have to borrow the 10th from you for a while so he can attend the meeting with us. Until then, take it easy."

After the 10th closed the car doors for Roland and Danton, he saluted Quin.

"I'll see you later, 10th," said Quin.

"Yes, Mr. High."

To avoid being seen near the zoo, Quin waited a few minutes for Roland, Danton, and the 10th to get off the island.

Chapter 13: Quin vs. Earnest 4

At the zoo dungeon, Quin listened at the top of the stairs for the voice he heard earlier.

While listening, he heard a low growling noise rising from below. Not knowing what to expect, Quin stepped back and prepared for an attack.

A familiar odor gave Quin the knowledge of who was approaching.

It was Earnest.

When Earnest came into view, he had transformed—about a foot taller, with noticeably longer and hairier arms. His facial features had become even more rat-like than before.

While distracted by the transformation, Quin was knocked down with a backhand.

When Quin rose, Earnest slowly moved towards him for another attack.

Despite Earnest's transformation, his attacks were still clumsy and uncoordinated. The two fought and Quin defeated Earnest just as easily as before.

Earnest lay unconscious on the ground.

Still determined to investigate the voice, Quin descended the stairs to the zoo dungeon.

There was no one there.

An empty water jar and a plate with breadcrumbs lay inside Earnest's vacant, open cell.

Quin returned upstairs to question Earnest about what happened, but Earnest was gone.

Earnest's scent led Quin outside the zoo's entrance.

When the two met, Earnest attacked again. Quin overpowered Earnest once more, leaving him unconscious again.

Quin tried to call Roland for advice, but there was no reception in the area.

Searching for Ashley would have been ideal, but Quin wasn't sure of Ashley's location and didn't want to leave Earnest alone. Quin considered dragging Earnest back down to another cell in the zoo dungeon, but he remembered the first cell's door was broken open and concluded that another cell would not hold Earnest.

As Quin pondered his next move, Earnest stood and growled.

"Earnest, who was talking to you while you were locked up? Who brought you that food and water?"

Earnest ignored Quin's question and attacked again.

The two fought again, but this time it was different. Earnest's attacks were not clumsy and uncoordinated like before. They were now refined and tactical.

Unable to quickly defeat Earnest, the fight spread across the exterior of the zoo. With each passing moment, Earnest's attacks became stronger. Quin felt as if he were fighting an entirely different person. Earnest was overpowering Quin.

Determined to win, Quin ignored how much damage he was taking until multiple strikes to his head caused him to fall to the ground. He was dizzy and unable to stand up. His body's healing was unable to keep up with his mounting injuries.

Earnest moved closer for another attack but froze a foot away from Quin, as if held by invisible chains. His body slowly rose off the ground, limbs thrashing wildly. Quin's relief came when he saw Ashley standing behind him.

"The Earnest I know could never best my youngest son. Who are you?"

With strained motions of her arms, Ashley's telekinesis hurled Earnest through the air and into the distance.

Quin, losing consciousness, felt darkness pulling him under as Ashley's figure blurred before his eyes.

Chapter 14: Angelic Betrayal

When Quin opened his eyes, he found himself lying on the couch in his hotel's lobby room. Ashley sat beside him, tilting a glass of blood into his mouth. She smiled silently as his gaze met hers.

"Earnest," Quin rasped. "He's stronger than me now, but I can still get him before he causes more damage."

"That is no longer just Earnest," Ashley replied softly. "A spirit has taken hold of him. The longer it stays in his body, the stronger it will grow. None of my other children or guards can make it back in time. You and I will have to stop him together—and quickly."

"If you hold him in place with your levitation, I can choke him out."

Ashley shook her head as she handed Quin another glass of blood. "Spirits resist my levitation. I learned from my nephew how to sing them out of humans. But I need time—and absolute focus for the song."

"Then I'll buy that time for you," Quin said, forcing himself upright to drink from the glass.

Ashley touched his shoulder, her voice soft but firm. "I'm thankful for your vigor. Know that if I fall in this fight, I can't protect you— or any of my children—on Judgment Day. Right now, you're my only protection."

Quin rose to his feet and clenched his fists. "I'm ready. Let's go before it gets worse."

Ashley gave a small nod, then pulled her cloak tighter around her shoulders. Together they stepped out of the hotel lobby and into the night air.

Fleeing animals, destroyed streetlights, and damaged trees guided Quin and Ashley to Earnest's location.

Earnest's body twitched violently, his eyes blazing with something not his own.

Ashley stepped out to address him, her voice low but firm. "You know The Son forbids you from possessing humans. Leave that body—because it belongs to me, and this island belongs to the Angel That Manifests."

Earnest's head tilted towards Ashley. When his mouth opened, the words that came were not his voice. "Jesus I know. Tansafo I know of. But who are you?"

Ashley leaned towards Quin without looking away from Earnest. "He's mocking us. Get ready."

Ashley raised her hand, and a nearby boulder tore free from the dirt. With a flick of her wrist, it sailed toward Earnest.

The possessed figure caught it midair with monstrous strength and hurled it back.

"Ashley!" Quin shouted, lunging forward. He caught the boulder with both arms before it could strike her, his knees buckling from the impact.

Quin charged at Earnest. Earnest swung wide with a backhand, but Quin ducked low, wrapped both arms around his opponent's legs, and drove him to the earth with a double leg takedown.

Quin tried to hold him down, straining every muscle, but Earnest snarled and powered back up, hurling Quin aside with a brutal punch that sent him crashing twenty feet away.

Before he could recover, Earnest leapt after Quin with his fist raised for a devastating blow.

Ashley snapped her hand out. A shattered tree branch flew towards Earnest's side, knocking him off balance.

Quin scrambled up, seizing the chance. He threw himself onto Earnest's back and locked his arms around his neck in a tight ground headlock.

Ashley's voice steadied across the chaos. "You're doing well, Quin. Hold him there—I'll begin."

Her words wove into the night, low and deliberate, the first syllables of the chant.

"The widow of forged imaginations.

The guilt that repels fire.

Gain loyalty to acknowledge the first wings of hunger."

Earnest's body convulsed until he freed himself from Quin's grip. Earnest then slammed Quin by the neck against a tree and began choking him. Quin gasped, clawing at the hand crushing his windpipe.

When Earnest heard Ashley's words, his head snapped towards her direction. His eyes burned with recognition as he released Quin and rushed at her.

Ashley's words faltered as she dodged a barrage of clawed strikes from Earnest. One savage swipe ripped the necklace from her throat, sending it clattering into the darkness.

Quin snatched up a rock and hurled it with all his strength. It struck the side of Earnest's head with a crack. Quin followed in with a desperate full-body tackle, sending Earnest several yards away from Ashley.

"You okay?"

Ashley pressed a hand to her bare throat. "I'm fine… except for the precious necklace he took."

"I noticed something—he ignored me when you started speaking."

"He knows what that chant will do. He will try to stop me at all costs."

"That gives me an idea. Start saying those words again."

Before Ashley could question him, Quin jumped into a nearby tree, masking his movements in the shadows.

Ashley steadied her breath and raised her voice again, continuing the chant.

The moment her words reached the air, Earnest roared and bolted toward her.

From above, Quin dropped down like a thunderbolt, clutching a sharpened branch. He impaled it through Earnest's back, using his own body weight to slam him into the ground, pinning him beneath the spear-like branch.

Ashley's eyes widened. "Excellent, my son. Hold him there!" She raised her arms and her voice rose in full force.

"The widow of forged imaginations.

The guilt that repels fire.

Gain loyalty to acknowledge the first wings of hunger.

Fight for rest!

Lawless for a human,

Advisable for the beasts.

Clarify! Obsess!

Debate with nature and judge the ancient sport!

Memories of the Angel That Shines: Kaihō no Tatsumaki!"

When Ashley finished speaking, a tornado lifted and swirled Quin and Earnest in the air. Waves of blinding lights radiated from the tornado's center, splintering trees in its path Quin instantly recognized the light—it was sunlight.

His entire body felt an intense burn that seeped into his bones. He could not escape the powerful winds nor remove his mask to stop the burning pain.

When the tornado subsided, Quin landed on the ground and was unable to get up. His entire body was covered in burn marks. Smoke still rose faintly from his body.

"Quin!" Ashley said, falling to her knees beside him. Her hands hovered over his burns, trembling, afraid to cause him more pain. "No... no, I didn't know there was sunlight inside... I didn't know."

Quin coughed, trying to force words out.

"Thank God you're still alive," Ashley cried, pressing her hand to his cheek in examination of his injuries.

"Did... we... win?" Quin asked in a raspy strain.

Ashley's gaze momentarily looked towards Earnest a few yards away. Earnest lay sprawled in the dirt, unmoving. His features returned to their normal human shape.

"He won't be moving for a few hours," she murmured, cradling Quin in her arms. "Right now, mommy needs to take care of you."

Ashley bathed Quin using the Innocent Inn's Jacuzzi and a wash brush on a pole. Quin wanted to resist, but he still couldn't move his body.

"I know this is embarrassing for you, but it's better that I do it rather than someone else."

Quin remained silent with the hope that the bath would end faster if he didn't respond.

"I'm responsible for this. If I had known that chant produced sunlight, I wouldn't have allowed you near it. The sunlight is only on the inside of the tornado, that's why I never noticed it before. I'm just thankful you survived."

After the bath was over, Ashley laid Quin on his hotel room's bed and poured a flask of blood into his mouth.

"It'll take you about a day to fully recover," Ashley explained.

"What about Earnest?"

"My guards should be back by now. We'll fetch him. Sleep until I return later. Keep your mask on to speed your healing."

Ashley returned to Earnest's location, accompanied by Ting and two Ambit Guards.

At her silent motion, the guards dragged Earnest upright and began striking him with sharp, disciplined blows. The assault ended only when one of them looped his belt around Earnest's neck, yanking him down like a chained dog until he knelt before Ashley.

"Earnest, can you still understand me?" Ashley asked, her tone measured as his body strained against the guard's grip.

"Me! Please let go! Gotta take care me mama."

"Broken English is better than none at all."

"Mama sick! Mama need me!"

"Your mother can move in with her sister. I'm sure they have a great deal of catching up to do."

Without warning, Ashley slapped Earnest across his cheek. The impact was so loud that it generated an echo and two of Earnest's teeth clattered to the ground.

Next, Ashley extended her hand, and Ting placed a loaded syringe in her palm. "Here is more of that addictive substance you'll spend the rest of your life chasing and working for," Ashley said coolly, driving the needle into his arm.

Earnest shuddered, his breath ragged.

Ashley turned to the guards. "Take him to a mirror and measure his intelligence. He will finally have his wish to remain with my daughter forever… as her slave!"

Quin awoke later that evening with some movement returned to his limbs, though he was still too sore to get out of bed.

Beside him sat a glass of blood and a vintage baby monitor.

Feeling offended by the baby monitor, Quin wanted to crush it but concluded that Ashley placed it there with sincere motives.

A few minutes later, Ashley arrived with a shoebox in her hands.

"Quin! Seeing you better brings me so much joy! How are you feeling?"

"There was a baby monitor put next to me while I was sleeping. Does everyone have a key to my room?"

Ashley placed the shoebox on a nearby drawer and came closer to Quin.

"Typically, only room service has a key. Me invading your privacy this time was only due to your injuries."

"I haven't seen anyone here for room service."

"I gave them time off. They'll resume working tomorrow afternoon. Earnest will be joining them to clean up the mess he caused."

Ashley began poking Quin on various parts of his body and used his reactions to judge how much pain he was in.

"Your soreness should be gone by morning. Before then, I want to see you smile. Take your mask off for a few moments."

After Quin did as he was told, Ashley handed him the shoebox.

Inside was a new cell phone and $50,000 cash.

An unyielding smile formed on Quin's face while he counted the stacks of bills.

"You'll be quite busy when you can move again. I'll leave you a car to use in this hotel's parking lot."

Ashley kissed Quin on the forehead and said, "I must get going."

Quin closed the shoebox and placed it to his side.

"Mother, before you go, I have to ask you something."

Ashley smiled at Quin and ran her hand in his hair. "Yes, my son."

"How do I know my fate won't be like Earnest's?"

Ashley looked at Quin for a long moment before she responded.

"Speaking frankly, Earnest was ignorant. He didn't even notice the mask I gave him was changing him into what he is now. Your skepticism guided you to search for the truth. I'm so proud you found it."

"I feel like there's something missing."

"Not asking or contemplating questions makes one vulnerable to deception. Your skills, intelligence, and desire for knowledge will protect you from becoming like him."

"I suppose I should finish school then."

"I encourage it. For now, let's wait until you've gotten a chance to visit the bank."

Ashley and Quin laughed together.

"Tomorrow morning," Ashley continued, "there is something I need you to retrieve from Jason Ward for me. I'll leave the location details inside the car along with the tea blood recipe."

Quin smiled as Ashley placed the mask back on his face.

As Ashley walked out of Quin's room, she levitated an envelope from Quin's desk and placed it on Quin's chest. It was a letter from Roland. Quin waited until she was gone before he read it:

To: My Younger Brother, Quin

From: Your Older Brother, Roland

Quin, these things I write to you so that you may not despair over your previous life. This letter is written with confidence that you will find full joy in your new family. For with this family, you are not a byproduct of instinct or poor decisions. With this family, you will know how and why you belong.

Few can articulate that there must be a reason to be confident. Through your mask you have been given a new life and a new reason to be confident.

It would not be wise to squander your new talents on someone who does not yet know nor fully understand themselves. You have no need to be like the others who endlessly compete for a lady's acceptance while she decides whom to reject. Use your mask to increase your value as a partner. Build an offer which no rival can compete with. Then you will be truly valuable in the eyes of your next love interest.

For what will you now say to young May? That you received a magical mask from someone who drinks blood?

Chapter 15: A New Family

The next morning, Quin could move his entire body freely again, and he felt stronger than before.

Quin used the car Ashley had left for him to drive to the bank to make his deposit. For the first time, Quin was not embarrassed to talk to the bank teller for fear of them seeing him broke. He even opened a savings account.

When the time came, Quin arrived at the same church in which he met Jason Ward. Only a few days had passed since Quin first met Earnest there, but Quin felt as if weeks went by.

Quin went into the church's conference room. It was the same room where Quin shook hands with Jason.

After a few minutes of waiting, Jason entered.

"Quin! Glad to see you again, or should I call you Uncle Quin?"

Quin took a second to process Jason's reference.

"Why—you're in the family?"

"Yes and no," laughed Jason, as he handed Quin a bottle of water. "I'm a descendant of one of your many siblings."

Quin stared at Jason, feeling awkward that an older man had just called him "Uncle."

"Liking the family so far?"

Quin smiled and responded, "Loving it!"

"I wish we had more time to chat, but today my team is conducting scholarship interviews, and you came for a Daylight Saving Crystal. I'll have one of the interviewees come and give it to you. We like to give them simple tasks to ensure they can follow instructions. This will kill two birds with one stone."

"Before you go, no one told me why Earnest wanted to steal that crystal from you."

"It's a crystal that prevents the use of Heaven's Time Zone. Earnest needed it to slow Ashley's children for his attack on her island. Hang tight and I'll send it in."

While waiting, Quin daydreamed about what he was going to do after he delivered the crystal.

I could get an apartment, but I already have a hotel and a motel. I don't know how long Ashley will let me use her car, so I could look into buying one of my own. I could get back into wrestling and be the strongest on the team! I could be the best at any sport, and if I get hurt again, my mask could just heal me like before! I could get endless scholarships! I could probably start a business! My parents could never be mad at me again with these plans! If I wanted to be funny, I could make more money and buy a house next door to them.

Quin's daydreaming was interrupted when the conference room's door opened again.

The person who entered made time seem to stand still. Quin's vision blurred while his heart alternated between stopping and racing. Breathing became difficult as emotions stiffened his body.

It was May.

"Quin?!"

Quin wanted to respond to May, but his throat felt as if spider webs were clogging it.

Only with a rush of adrenaline from watching May get closer was Quin able to move. He reached for his water and drank it.

"You look different, Quin!"

Quin choked from drinking his water too fast.

"I startled you. I didn't expect to see you during my interview today!"

After the coughing ceased, Quin called her name, "May!"

"Your ankle got better a few weeks ahead of schedule."

"May, what happened?"

"The donor I met arranged for me to interview for this scholarship so I could finish school."

"I mean with us."

May took a seat near Quin and released a heavy sigh. "It was the best decision for both of us."

"You're all I was thinking about."

"I know it was hard for you. I didn't want to make it worse. I was hoping you would see you're better off without me."

"May, I don't even know what happened."

"It was a chance to get your family back and your life together. I was distracting you."

"You would have stayed with me if I had my life together?"

"I wanted to grow and learn my potential. Now we have the chance to find out who we are and who we want to be. Hard to do that when you're so broke you're too afraid to check your own bank account."

Quin remained silent while he reflected on his conversations with Roland.

"I heard you work for the city now. That's a step up. We are both doing better in our new lives."

Quin inhaled deeply to steady his heart rate and responded, "You're right. I have a lot ahead of me."

"Yes! I could even introduce you to the donor! His name is Roland Ambit. He could even help you."

Quin laughed. "No thanks, that's okay."

"I'm glad you see it differently now. I needed to get that off my chest. The interviewers told me to give you this lockbox."

Quin failed to notice that May brought with her a large metal box with a combination lock. Quin took the box and spoke his final words to May.

"Thank you. I know your interview will go well."

When Quin returned to Ashley's Island, he met with Ashley in the Innocent Inn's parking lot.

Ting and Earnest were with her. Earnest washed Annalisa's car while Ting supervised him with a taser wand.

Ashley hugged Quin and took the lockbox from him.

"Did you find closure with your past today, son?"

Quin silently stared at Ashley for a few moments before realizing what she was referring to. Ashley looked back at him and lifted a cup of blood to her mouth and drank.

"You—you really did force May and me to talk again?"

Ashley lowered the cup and smiled.

"Unlike most parents, I don't have to constantly scream that I'm your mother to compel you. I can influence your actions without you even knowing."

"I get that now. You did it for my best interests. Thanks to you, I can see that I am beyond May now."

"Why do you feel that way now?"

Quin took a deep sigh while Ashley took another sip of blood from her glass.

"You've given me the power to start over, become better, and to get the best. I no longer have to settle for less. May still hasn't figured out what she wants to do with her life yet."

Ashley laughed, revealing her fangs for the first time.

"I told you a child of mine deserves better in life. I mean that for everything, not just a partner. Never forget, the more options you have, the better your life will become. You now have options. What would you like to do next, my youngest son?"

Looking at his mask, Quin grinned broadly. "I'd like to meet the rest of my new family!"

"That's wonderful news because I need you to rescue your kidnapped brother!"

The End

Thank you for reading

ASHLEY'S CHILDREN

For the comedy version of Quin's story, check out the manga version!

ASHLEY'S CHILDREN

Quin's Manga 1

Written By Drep Code
Art By Ultrafrogz

Available where books are sold. Scan the QR code for details!

www.AshleysChildren.com

Author Bio

Drep Code, born in Michigan, served in the U.S.
Navy from 2011 to 2015. He moved to Hawaii in
2015 to study Criminal Justice and Psychology at
Chaminade University.

Inspired by evolutionary psychology and world
events, he now writes fiction novels and comics
that focus on relatable realism. Published by Bird
Feeders Media, his works are available on
platforms where book are sold.

Follow Drep Code on Instagram @TheDrepCode
for updates and more!

Scan for links

www.ingramcontent.com/pod-product-compliance
Lightning Source LLC
Chambersburg PA
CBHW071520170626
46811CB00007B/2913